M000309499

DATE

IN THE YEAR OF LONG DIVISION

DAWN

Stories

RAFFEL

Alfred A. Knopf   New York   1994

IN

THE

YEAR

OF

LONG

DIVISION

This Is a Borzoi Book
Published by Alfred A. Knopf, Inc.

"We Were Our Age" appeared in The Iowa Review;
"The Other R's" in New Letters; *"The Trick" in*
Epoch; *"The Seer" in* Gulf Coast; *"Disturbances in*
the Night" in Confrontation; *"Migration" in*
American Letters *and* Commentary; *"Something Is*
Missing of Yours," "In the Year of Long Division,"
"City of Portage," "Table Talk," "Seeds in Public
Places," "Secrets of Breeding," "Somewhere near Sea
Level," "Nightjars," "Up the Old Goat Road," and
"Two If by Sea" in The Quarterly.

Library of Congress Cataloging-in-Publication Data
Raffel, Dawn.
In the year of long division : stories / by Dawn Raffel.
p.   cm.
ISBN 0-679-41581-5
I. Title.
PS3568.A372I5   1994
813'.54—dc20   93-43940   CIP

Manufactured in the United States of America

First Edition

FOR MICHAEL

I am deeply grateful to Gordon Lish. I want also to thank Christine Schutt, Heywood Hale Broun, Marsha Spyros of the New York Public Library, my dear friends Cindy Schweich, Emma Segal, and Etta Jacobs, and the editors of the literary magazines who first published these stories. And my family! Brendan! May you thrive.

CONTENTS

We Were Our Age   3

The Other R's   9

Something Is Missing of Yours   18

In the Year of Long Division   23

City of Portage   30

The Trick   36

Table Talk   48

Seeds in Public Places   52

The Seer   55

Somewhere near Sea Level   67

Nightjars   73

Secrets of Breeding   95

Disturbances in the Night   98

Up the Old Goat Road   103

Migration   107

Two If by Sea   114

IN THE YEAR OF LONG DIVISION

WE

WERE

OUR

AGE

DUKE'S brother died under the ice in spring, the season I met Duke. The other kid survived—shivering, fat-lipped, the instigator, littler. A miracle, the search team said. Just a hurt front tooth, a gash, a stitch. A boy's likely story. This is what I heard, but not from Duke.

Duke said, "Go."

Duke said, "Ladies first, please."

Rock, rock, gap, stone-cold to the lighthouse—Duke and I were spiny in the dark. Weeds swam up. Weak sunk stars, a lap, suck, and bubble. The usual. Lake and pier. Us and us. Month after month.

Duke was always finding things to skip across to who knew where.

August.

Pinkness hovered.

A school was in the ebb of the tide, bellied over easy.

"Ready or not," Duke said.

We were our age.

Fishing was the only sport in our town. How it was. Pick. Any house in our town was any house in our town. Any wind in our town was the wind in our town. Down was down. Queasy was a way of life. Bored to crackers, snap, *kerplunk.*

That Duke was smart. Had a flat-out daddy, elbow-room. Had boxes' worth of weatherproof clothes, size close enough. Had any-purpose pockets.

Maybe I obliged. The least I could do.

All the talk in our town was talk, talk, talk. That, no this. Rain, no shine. More, no less. Pardon me, ma'am.

Duke said, "No news is good news."

Quiet, that was me. To a fault. Sneakers on the rocks. A torn boy's poncho, blue, somebody else's breath in the hair. Braids—loose. Skin—pale. Sky—slow and dangerous.

The lighthouse was an eyesore. Fenced to match. Wood—swollen. *Tender* is what I would have liked to have said. Gulls—posted.

Signs ignored by us.

Single file in the evening, Duke and I.

Ready and not.

NO one was allowed to go beyond a certain point.

Certainly not with Duke.

• • •

COMMON—the names they had. The kid. The brother. Had had. Short. Like Duke.

I was the kind of girl to write lists:

Tar.

Rope.

Bone.

Glass.

Hook, I think.

Nylon.

Sand.

Peau de soie.

Chunk.

In the night, on the skin, erasable, rinsable. Or only in the skull.

Imagine.

THE smell of these things was a whole other story. I could be that discreet.

HERE is how it was another way in our town, in any icy season (puddly fall; the holidays—glint, glint and breakage, scouting for the egg in the shy grass): scraped and dug. Glare. Any house in our town was sealed. Any words in our town were used. Any sorrow underfoot.

On the lake: red right encrusted. Pier—tied off.

In the mudrooms: boots and salty rinds. Skin and wool, wet. The weight of skin and wool, wet. The feel of skin and wool, wet; not to mention the smell— pale nose scrunched and sunk in a crook, the way a girl would do.

News—dredged.

Coffee—black.

Any window had somebody waiting behind it. Wet air seeped.

In the square of our town: bank, bait and tackle. Gulls and bread. Rx. The hill. The wayward strands of the light.

In the churchyard: Duke. Duke's sobered-up or anywise daddy, scrubbed. Chin—coarse, perhaps. A kid with a kid's common name. Me.

This could almost be a scene in our town.

SIX in one—any scene in our town. Before.

THE kind of girl I was, I could swallow ink. Paper, too. A hangnail, laces, possibly a fin, a dove, a jack-in-the-box, cement, and, with a little urgent purpose, someone's dry wrap, a buoy.

We had local standards. Had to.

I could have won a cup.

SIX in one.

After.

ANY conversation could go like this:

"Go."

"Ladies first, please."

Lapse.

Or this: "No news is good news."

Lapse.

Or this: "Feel?"

Lapse.

Or this: Lapse.

Any lapse in our town was mine. Any pause. Any possible yes.

But only sort of.

SUMMER—easy. So much was obvious, stripped of the cloak of the ice, salt. Duke was Duke. Fish washed up. I was a girl who could see through skin, but only to the bones. Natural events took place. Bells rang. Supper cooled. Corn turned sweet, got picked in another Middle West.

In the mudrooms: mud.

On the doors: screens, gripe in the hinges. Someone on the pier hooked a sock—size boy's obvious, same as the one that got away.

Duke had a knack. He could tie a tourniquet. Said so.

Heat could wobble. Did so.

Lightning struck us dopey.

In the square of our town: speculation, counter-talk. Knee-bang on Formica. Anybody's saucer pooled.

By Fridays, anything a body could abide—by rasher, by platter, by bucket, by stretcher: potatoes, potatoes, slaw, slaw, slaw, and something burning.

The keeper of the lighthouse drank. "According to the actual physical record," as Duke's daddy told it.

Duke said, "All you can. And after that, then some."

Duke's daddy by September got a gut.

I WAS a girl who wanted silk.

Our lake was great. Could have been an ocean.

Under the surface, everything shone.

HERE is how it was in the night with Duke, alone on the pier, a stone's short throw from the world: We were ourselves. A keeper could blink. I could swallow gristle and muscle; oh, that bloody reek—my heart.

Fell in. Likely. Urge and rage, a boy and girl, and once in, over and over, rage and urge, diving for the thing that would not save us.

THE

OTHER

R'S

THE R's—the other R's, not us—had something the matter with their baby. In the summer in the after-dinner light of our street, when Mother and the mothers with babies would be sitting, two and three and four, to cool on cool stoops, to knit and clack or beg and share a lipsticked cigarette, yarns puffing out of bundles at their feet, the arms of sweaters, loose, crissed across a waist, a mother's belly, a neck—hair rolled; when the babies would be sucking or asleep, Mother and the mothers drinking drinks of bottled pop, tree-tied tires would be swinging, red flies lighting, and poor Mr. next-door M, bushed, being pulled on a leash, one of the two of the boarder nurses hooked up, honked for, riding out of uniform again with men, and children: G's, J's, us—C and DR, clovering and fighting and whuffing picky milky balls of weed off weeds, fathers hosing, sweating; when all the goings-on of our street, our lawns, would be going on and on, the

R's—the other R's—would not, would never, once, come out.

Their house was draped. Tight. Tucked in on the block.

We were made to snoop.

He, Mr. R—not our father—could be seen in the mornings leaving, never coming back. She would be out in the high heat of day, a mother buttoned and bunchy in the elbows, a mother not ours, wearing saddle shoes, a mother passing other mothers' houses, bumping the carriage on the sidewalk, stepping on the cracks.

The carriage was a dark, hooded thing.

We would hang back to watch—quiet, drawn.

We had heard the priest had come.

We had heard it was supposed to be a boy, this R baby neighbor the nurses swore they had each seen, that the soft nurse said she had bathed once, that the pocked nurse vowed was feeding, gaining its weight.

We would be a fat-tongued gaggle, looking at the sparkle in cement. We would be burnt-nosed, flat feet thonged. We would be thick into shrubs, cross, scratchy in the burrs.

We saw wheels. Spokes and pleats were what we saw, the carriage's ribs, her looking in—in and in. She would be touching the hood of the carriage, touching crushed net. She would be moving her lips or else looking at us: a sticky and streaky, scab-kneed clan—G's all jam on the fingers, shirttails, somebody chewing on a braid, BG not much but ears, and minus teeth, three hipless J's, each in the next J up's old last year's clothes, Peggy in the middle with the asthma, picked-on, C and I our own can't-pry-us-apart, don't-try-it selves. Or could have been she didn't even know us.

Her eyes were pale, and she had pale lank hair, pale lips, the palest of voices.

What did she utter? We did not hear.

We had never heard crying from deep in the carriage.

WE had heard it had a heart.

(How could it not?)

MOTHER and the mothers would stand in heat to knock at the storm-doored door, fixing their faces, smoothing their hair in the smeared, distorting glass. They carried covered dishes: small foods, creamed to soothe—peas, corn; sweet pie steaming through a forked crust; loaves and loaves wrapped up in shine.

Mother brought a spoon. Mrs. G brought an animal, bright-eyed, stuffed; a musical mobile of fat-finned and fat-tailed creatures of the water.

Mrs. M brought a son. He was a junior version of Senior, always appearing to be chewing something used. He was there to weed, his mother said. He would help to prune, she said, and dump.

Declined.

No one brought a thing conforming to the body—darlingly footed, tenderly cowled—nothing blushingly pink or baby blue.

. . .

HOW could they not? It was impossible not to, really: They compared—sitting on stoops, perspired in kitchens, stirring, pouring—the mothers did—over the clothes-lines—"What did you see?"—engaging the sprinklers—"She said what?"—wiping a nose, a blotchy cheek, changing the babies—"You?" "You?"

It was, for us, a humming. We were busy as mothers, C and I. Screens banged. Pops dripped. Rules were set, according to the ordinary governance of children—tap, tap, rotten egg and last one in; a dare, a threat—and always leaving Peggy wheezing (balled-up face enraged).

The shame of it, the mothers said. That we heard. That was clear. Not a minute in the nursery of those sad R's. Not a coffee in the kitchen, a peek in the hall. And on the doors, the mothers said, storm glass still.

"No breeze," said Mother, anchoring pigtails. "Not a lick," she said, "of air, and it so hot. Dank."

"That blinding smell," said Mrs G. "Ideas?"

There were ideas.

There were serious pieces of mind.

"The woman," Mrs. M said, "has my pretty tray."

"My bowl," Mrs. G said. "Not that it hurts me."

Someone was screaming.

"If I were Mrs. R," Mrs. J said.

Someone was howling.

"Stop right now," Mrs. M said. "Someone could lose the use of an eye."

"If you were her," Mother said.

"Do you want to be punished?" Mrs. M said.

"If," Mother said.

"Well," Mrs. J said, "I just can't think what, if you know what I mean."

THE nurses knew. They were openly privy to the what was what. "No damage to the lungs," the soft nurse said. "Nothing the matter with the wind," she said. "It breathes," she said. She'd had it all firsthand: She was dating a doctor. The pocked nurse supposedly told Mr. next-door M, Mother said, the trouble was, it lived.

"PATIENCE of a saint," Mother said.

Our street smelled mowed.

"*He* is like to drink," Mrs. J said to Mother.

"Someone is listening," Mother said.

Peggy was pinned.

Mrs. J was cutting piping. Her spools were on the stoop. She was making a frock, its one-of-a-kindness some kind of consolation for Peggy. ("And where will Peggy wear it?" Mother had said.)

"The shame of it," Mrs. J said. "Out all night, he is," she said. "Think of it."

(I thought of it—a man, not our father, in the night, in the night-lit glow of smeary rooms, nakedly smoking.)

"Ladies," Mother said.

C was scratching. Peggy coughed. I was peeling skin. We were bitten and reddened from the long, oiled days; spare nights pitched-tented in the side yards, spooking Peggy, parched.

Our breathing grew ragged.

"Count your blessings," Mother said.

Hood, pleat, rib, rib—we were gawking witnesses.

"The shame," Mrs. J said.

For there it was: Mrs. R was laboring—crack, crack—doubling almost over the terrible carriage's terrible cargo.

I DID not see the candles. I did not see the gown. I did not see the priest. I did not see the long black car in the light of the morning. I did not see Mother. I did not see the fingers of my sister, digging—nails in the heat of my flesh. I did not see the earth. I did not see the marks. I was playing blind, eyes covered with linen, the day they buried Peggy.

MUST we continue? Summer continued. ("No one could help it," the soft nurse said, speaking of Peggy. "Better off," the pocked nurse said. "Don't you think?") The mothers baked. Sweetly, and ever so gently, Mrs. G inquired as to Peggy's piped frock, which frock, as it happened, Peggy was wearing wherever Peggy was. They had closed the box.

"There must be a reason," Mother said.

"There will be an angel," the soft nurse said.

"There will be roses," the pocked nurse said, "with plenty of thorns."

Roses there were: thorny, snitched. Someone, it seemed, was stealing from the gardens of our street. Willy-nilly. Violets shabby and rotting, limp petunias, daisies bald as "loves-me-not," the weekend blooms of Mr. M, dog-eared stalks and watered ragweed—rank and flung they lay, weeping and stinking on the stoop of the bereaved.

"Why, why, why?" Mrs. J said. "There is no sense."

Someone, the mothers agreed, with an unfit mind was darting about in the dead of the night.

Days grew shorter. Days-old bread appeared. Flat cake, greenish biscuits—ugly. "Why in the world?" said Mrs. J, dressed in black, her face pinched. She would not bend. She would not pick these up, these ugly things, untouchable, delivered to the very stoop of her house.

"What else?" Mother said. "What in the wide world else will the woman have to suffer?"

This: the heaping plate outside her door, identified as something belonging to Mother.

THERE was a mystery here: The carriage was missing.

"Bite your tongue," C said.

Nobody answered the storm-doored door. The mothers knocked. Mrs. M took to kicking.

What had Mother not got back? the mothers said.

"My bowl," Mrs. G said. "Not that I notice."

Day leaked into day leaked into day, and no one saw it—pleat nor rib, bulging hood. (The more the unseeable thing was not seen on our street, the more I nearly saw it: a speck in my eye, a flicker, there in our yard, there in our house, a tightness down in my throat, and there in our room, a shadow.)

Oh, I was tired, yawning.

"Seal your lips," my sister said.

"What did she see?" I wanted to know.

Why, the soft nurse might have said, had Peggy, according to a certain dated doctor, run? What was Peggy doing in the dark, alone, where she had been found?

(I am afraid to think, still, of what the pocked nurse might have said.)

"Who shut the windows?" Mother said.

"What did she see?" I said to my sister.

Night leaked into night.

"Not healthy," Mother said.

"Who?" my sister said.

"Someone has entered the cupboards," Mother said.

"Then speak for yourself," C said.

Head bowed, in whispers, faint, through screen, I would confess to Mr. M, mourning his garden.

"What do you have to say?" Mother said.

I did not sleep.

C, I think, must not have slept. "Go away," she said.

There were the sounds of our unsound nights.

There was the question the mothers had for Mother: What had Mother lent?

IN the night, our street, our houses vanished. Whole, lost. One by one, two and three; and three of us, there would be three of us, nightly moving, shut of our houses, out of our tents—nights, nights, nights. A lone seam, milky, rising, coming as if from an unseen flue—we would see it rise. We would let it lead us, two abreast and one behind, and one night, one of us forcibly piggied at a window. One

shriek. Four arms, four legs, two heads—nights, nights—
unable to look in the face of the other: That was us. All
there was was this: the noise of our nights—a whimper in
a torn-through garden, snores, a moan—love, I think—of
a woman or a man, a father, anyone's father; our rent
breath, a crying, pallid and rising, almost a keening, rising, the falling and the falling of our feet.

SOMETHING

IS

MISSING

OF

YOURS

THEY are burning the leaves out back, at the edge of the yard—far back enough for the father's peace of mind from the house. The father, of course, is the one who is taking care of the burning. The daughter, having done her share of raking and bunching, is standing aside in the shrubby bramble, hands slid into her loden pockets, watching the house for signs.

"Smell," the father says.

"I'm cold," the daughter says. "I can see my breath."

"That's impossible. Look at these reds," the father says. "Elm leaves maybe. Maple."

"I have a burr in my shoe," the daughter says.

The father jiggers the leaves with a length of branch,

scaring up cindery flecks. "You're sounding just like her," the father says. "Really. You know what that's liable to spell?"

"No, I don't," the daughter says.

"Then too bad for you," the father says.

THE mother is lying in bed smoking filterless cigarettes filched from the father's jacket pocket. A windfall of linens—wash towels, kerchiefs, lingerie—is scattered around her, wrung out, reused. She has twist-top bottles the color of some kind of syrup in bed with her, too, and same-colored stains of it, a few spoons needing washing, a mateless sock, a thermometer, which does not work, a bu-tane lighter, a wristwatch—scratched—pumpkin seeds, makeup, the crusts of toast.

"Tell me," the mother says to the daughter, who stands by her bedside. "What time is it? What were you all that time up to together back out there?"

"Just upkeep is all," the daughter says.

"Save it," the mother says. "Hand me that lipstick."

"Where?" the daughter says.

The mother blows a smoke ring. "Make a wish," she says. "Some color becomes me, your father said. Once."

"It would," the daughter says. "Now."

"If what?" the mother says.

"Beats me," the daughter says. "Anyway, suppertime's coming up soon."

"Again?" the mother says.

. . .

NOTHING is out in the yard except for what rightly, by nature, belongs there. The usual stirrings—flappings, flickering things. A slight shudder of brier. A rumor of frost. Tall grasses and weedy things. Garden and yard tools dirtied with earth. There are scootings and squirrelings. Whiffings. Hoots. Cool acorns, pine cones, thistle and fluff. Things that drift down slowly, softly. Scratchings. Markings. Tender signs—if one is looking to see them.

"HE says to stop raiding his pockets," the daughter says to the mother, who taps an ash off on the wadded bedding by way of response. "Do you know what you're doing is asking for trouble?"

"I know what I know," the mother says.

The daughter turns and looks out the bedroom window.

"Do you?" the mother says.

"Couldn't you pick this place up?" the daughter says.

"What kind of an answer is that?" the mother says.

THE daughter says to the father, "It's raining—and that's not the half of it, either."

THE daughter believes that the father often enters her room at times when she is not there, and that he opens her dresser drawers. She imagines the father handling fabric, possibly running a finger the delicate length of a seam.

She is of the impression that sooner or later the father

slips himself into her bed, but not to rest. Instead, she envisions the father regarding the ceiling above his head, maybe taking note of the slightest beginnings of water damage there.

THE daughter can never seem to sleep in her bed at night. Night after night, she lies alert, aware of the bedclothes touching her skin. Looking up, in the light of the moon coming in through the parted window lace, what the daughter sees on the ceiling is next to nothing.

THE father has followed the daughter into the kitchen, where she is setting the kettle down on the range flame.

"There's work needs doing outside," the father says.

"Maybe later," the daughter says.

"When?" the father says.

The daughter yawns. "Search me," she says. "I'm all the time so sleepy."

"Tea is the ticket," the father says.

"I wonder," the daughter says, "why would a person talk in their sleep."

"Plenty of sugar," the father says. "And milk."

The daughter opens a carton and sniffs. "God, is this evil," she says.

"Who do you know who talks in their sleep?" the father says, shutting the flame off.

"Nobody," the daughter says. "That's who."

• • •

THE daughter has fallen asleep in the mother's bed, with her arms around the mother, and with most of the mother's soiled belongings pushed over to one side.

THE daughter is out behind the house, in the place where the ground is scarred. The air is crisp and still, and there is just the slightest motion of a curtain as the daughter tends to burning what she is burning one by one.

IN

THE

YEAR

OF

LONG

DIVISION

THEY were always breaking bones across the street. Knuckled and fisted, those boys had bruised voices that traveled, raised. We could hear them in the alley in the night behind our house, the curtains swelling in a room still shared. We lay in bed awake and listened. Brothers, they did it to themselves, our mother said, to each other, she supposed; a leg, a crushed elbow, knees—deserved. We were female in our house. We cracked the windows for air, my sister said, for better winter breathing.

Days, we saw those boys in the sun, in snow, pants slit up the seams; the quick glint of a splinted finger, foam. Our neighbors were whistling, snow-slinging, crutching.

Their socks were rough and thermal. Wool, maroon—the grimed red of a scab where a shoe was gone. We thought the casts were dyed. We saw wobbles and scribbles. Names were named in ink.

At first, we could not tell those boys apart or, in the holler and tilt of them in motion, just how many of them there really were. We were strangers to their injuries. Girls. We dressed in mostly purses and dresses, straps flat and narrow down the hollows of our shoulders, straight, neat—not a collarbone banged, not a square patch of bandage at an eye to keep the eye tight shut.

The boys' mother was missing a breast, our mother said. She said, "Those boys are good for trouble, fatherless boys like those. Look out."

We looked out from indoors. Nose-to-glass, we looked, fogging, we looked, through the damp of our exhalations, downstairs, upstairs, piggyback—we saw scenes through see-through curtains, a shadow boxing with a shade, something bubbled, tubside—every which way we could find to look, we did; one and the other, and once—or was it twice?—both, in a wash, shriveled and skin-shedding, soaked in looks of bathroom-window-frosted boy. Rings ringed the tub. We left smudges in our wake of who knew what.

Rust. Spit. Lotion. Spit and polish, spray and wax, and gabardine going dotty in a closet, smells, plugs, the smell of Mother, and starch, and rutted underfoot wood, patent leather and nails, bleach, blood, gum and balls of hair balls in the drain—this was our house.

We girls were squealing-clean.

Inside, we knew our number. We could count on it—wholesome, even, and Mother made three.

We were shy of nothing so much as the facts.

We were not of one mind. Those underhanded boys, our mother said, were throwing rocks and sticks in our direction. They were capable of damage. They had matches, those boys, and stink bombs and canes. Their wrists were thick and knobby. Growing boys, they were winging grenades at the stoops on both sides of the street, and there was recent talk of missiles.

"Poor, poor her," our mother said, speaking of the mother of the boys. "It's in the glands," our mother said. "Pits—pits of apricots," our mother had been overheard to say into the phone when we were busy overhearing. "Glands. . . . Bananas. . . . A holy hill of beans," our mother said, "and not a man in clear sight."

But whose heart was beating hardest?

This was in the year of falling and falling and falling snow. Day and night, night and day and afternoon—it did not matter. There were drifts above the height of our imaginings. Sisters, not twins, we were not the same in body and build, but in the alley in back, our booted feet went sliding higher in tandem than the various places where otherwise our heads might more rightly have been.

It was the year of hocus-pocus and underwater voodoo—"Do you do it, too?" my sister said—and making angels on our backs. We leaked. Boots and tights and shins, all dripping. Our jackets had been lacking. Slushy, and full of the smell of ourselves and of synthetic, sopping fleece, we poured our sorrows out to Mother. We exploded in sneezes, emptied our purses, slid weak ankles in the stream of the tap.

"Lukewarm," our mother said, and not, as we had thought, hot.

The drain choked. We were mottled and tender and to blame for flowing over. We should have worn pants, our mother said.

Girls will be girls. We should have worn gloves for making pristine bricks.

Because those boys were building fortresses and hospitals. Headlong, in a rush of fresh construction, there was one of those boys erecting bases and silos and hotels with special access—or so we thought we'd heard.

It was the hard packing snow with slivered ice. It was good, we believed, for inflammations. It had quieted the air to punch-drunk.

Our ears rang.

Blue, in the insubstantial hours under covers, stray syllables between us were strange and often lost. Long halls wandered window-lit alone turned to blind and empty spaces, hushful and soft, and holding only the soft sounds of Mother on a late, blind line.

We sisters swapped our beds. Lonely, we took to stuffing pillows up high beneath our dresses, admired the effect and learned to squint. Mysterious machinery appeared beneath our windows. Those busy, industrious, and backbreaking boys were in possession of equipment of a glorious kind. We were glowing in reflection. But no one had a shovel.

We were snowed deep in.

School had been suspended, and this in the year of

long division and remedial enrichment and lunch and petty cloakroom theft.

"Twice removed," our mother said to who knew who and spoke of travel.

"Oh," our mother said another time. "Oh, for the sun to heal the ache."

We were hitting our studies at the sink.

"I should have been an old Chelsea dog," our mother said. Or maybe not, for there was racket and distortion. We were occupied in brushing up on new zones of shame. We were crackerjack geographers. "Water, water everywhere," my sister said, and this without a map.

The snowy street was in relief. It was a vision of bridges and hangars, struts. It was immaculate traction. There were viaducts and overpasses, loop-the-loop ramps. A scaffold-shadowed boy was propped hunching in a chairlike contraption, inventing the wheels. We saw a hat-snatching scuffle and a split-and-whistle wrestle on a bank. There was a flash of something foreign.

"Pity, pity her," our mother said about the missing other mother, and spoke often of invasion and vitamins and cysts and escalation and nausea and pity.

There were more of those boys. There were more of those boys. There were more of those boys, of all ages and stripes. Everywhere we looked, those boys were there and there and there. On certain of their heads, the hair was white. They were limping and coughing and clinging from the rafters, faces pressing fleshy to the glass of our house. They had flattened their noses. They were armed. They were shooting down the chimney and pounding on the milk chute and dropping like flies by the slot for mail.

"Someone's buzzing at the door," my sister said. We were freshening up. In the mirror, we could see a strange relation. We could feel it in our marrow. We were not quite girls.

And where was Mother? Where was Mother in the hour when we needed her most?

Because the world was full of boys, and of full-fledged fellows. There were gentlemen of industry and corporals and serious lawyers. This would be no ordinary shirtsleeve street fight. A marching band was marching into view.

There was a rumble up and coming.

Brass horns blatted out "The Star-Spangled Banner." There were body bags and drums, maneuvers. The air was turning misty and ballistic. We could smell it. An ambulance was screaming. Someone was insisting he was Swiss.

But who could answer? It was impossible to think. It was a blizzard of plaster and limbs. Clothes and blood and nails all flew, in and out of the house, in hotels and planes and hospitals—who cared and who could tell? The telephone was dead. A taste was in our mouths of something other than ourselves and we could sniff it on each other. Things were vanishing from inside out. Halls, the tub, the alley—there were bodies in the room in which we slept, a hit and rustle in a closet, and skeletons falling bone on bone on gabardine. Fur, sticks, bats, and holy hell came hailing down and down and down around our heads.

And then it was quiet.

And then it was level.

Silent, save a trickle.

The fellows—the men—were all gone. It appeared

that they had packed up their bags and their cities and their tools and up and left.

We waited.

We knitted.

We received a scribbled card that said to wait. For they were staking out the globe. They were laying in foundations. They were rolling the steam to pave the milk white way, to pave the dazzling path for what was closest to our hearts, for what was swelling and floating and building—brain and heart and marrow—for the strangers, the sharers, quickening and kicking in the dark beneath our skin.

CITY

OF

PORTAGE

THE widow did not want to go in the boat. She said so, too, she did. Twice in the rapids, the widow said, that sun too hot, that Peshtigo water chafing her with rust and biting silt—bloat, the widow said, the river up, the boat bark weak.

But the man appeared not to have heard her. He was bailing something puddled out of the hull, spilling it onto the loose earth.

"We ought, too, to think of the boy," the widow said.

"Ought what?" the man said.

"Him not half-grown," the widow said, "the Peshtigo drunk, him—the boy—head-over-heels into water, rock, blood," she said. "Bloody, bloody river."

"A story, that," the man said, not stopping bailing.

She would rather not have looked. The man's hands, the widow knew, were rough, the webs of flesh blistered.

"That boy was no account of yours," the man told her.

"Don't fill your head. That boy was thick. That boy most likely must have jumped."

The widow squatted down to gunwale level. No, she said, no. She had eyes. She was not so thick herself or dim or gray as all that. So he could save his *p*'s and *j*'s, she said, whatever else, excuses, rancid wet birch lunch, strokes. She had her sturdy canvas shoes. She had a widow's intuition, cash. No more questions needed, please, she said. It was decided.

"Can't," the man said.

"Can't?" the widow said.

The man was doing something with the nails of his fingers.

She stood.

"Can't get to there by overland alone," the man said.

There was a sound the widow heard and could not place. There was wetness in the bends of her elbows, a low-boiled feeling deep between her breasts. "And what about the burden of portage?" she said.

"Justice," the man said. "Blind."

Then she would steer, the widow said. No questions, please, or boyish sciences of his of navigation. No sir, the widow said. It was decided.

BY talk? he said. By chance? he said. By devil double-daring? Would she holler them across? the man said. Take it sheer will or miss? the widow thought she heard him say. By echo, did he say? Had he said echo?

. . .

THE river's hue was something rare, the widow saw. It was the riverish hue of each rare, raging thing and thing's shadow, each shadowy submergence rising up against the boat. Dark under-paddle Peshtigo, the widow saw, was flush, ored, flushing under her and minerally lit against a widow's washy stroke. No dumb rush, this, the widow saw, no passive mincing brook; this was mineral intelligence, a sparkle like a smart glint of eye, a knower's wink she would as soon have not seen. This was mettle, ire, an unmined bed of metal husbandry below the widow's body. She rocked; she listed; she listened to the rap against the birch, against the rocks, the rapid rising sluice, the rising Peshtigo a hard hue and scratch against a parched-white side, against a hull, against a widow's nettled passage. The man was a foment of foamish motion up in front. He was a mannish birchy sound from a direction she did not wish to steer to, to hear from—down, a wraparound of blind-dark curve of rapid dark, dark as unbroken day and sucking dark orish rush, a dark crack against a dumb cut of stump, a stand of reed, ragged edges of the overhangs of sere-dark shore, red knolls and rottish woods, soft, swelled, the opened second-sighted flesh of a boy, the mudded dell, the swaddled shores of Mother Leary's shedded unlanterned dark. Leery O'Leary of the unquenched flame, of flamish lullabye and Peshtigoish bedtime tale, the boat a cradle in the rocks, unbound, a cradled falling, falling. The corded flesh was singing. The widow was puckered and crooked and raw—dark Peshtigo an unseasoned salt against the skin, whetting, sharp, a liquored lick, a trickle tunneling the breasts and chas-

tened narrows of the legs, a puddled hold of natatorial intelligence as yet not plumbed, a dampened sun, a watered
absence sunk beneath a widow's loose and tendered flesh.
She was soaked, drenched, drained. Undrunk. She was
widowed. She did not wish to rest. She did not want to
speak. She did not want to see to concede to the man, to
the boat that she was night-blind lost, that she was going
near to gone.

THE Peshtigo was quick.

WAS she watching at all? the man wanted to know. The
Peshtigo was not the Kinnickinnic, he said. Was she carrying a grudge?

"Nicolet," the widow said.

Would she look? the man said. Pay attention to the
river? Was she even half-trying to steer, to hold to course?

Need he ask? She could not even swim, the widow
said, much less, and neither could he—boyish missing
Nicolet, the widow said, and, in fact, she did not wish to
start.

"Please," the man said. "Not now."

She could see that he was doing something scraping,
some scrapey-sounding thing along a rib of the boat.

"And what of the wife?" the widow said.

"Port," the man said.

This was important.

"Did Nicolet leave a wife?" the widow said. "Was

there one, a water widow? And you?" the widow said. The man's shirt, she saw, was wetted clear to glistening in back.

Was she deaf? the man said. Could she follow a simple direction?

Listen. What she was, the widow said, was sore. Her elbows were achy, her knuckles, palms. They were not even French, the widow said. Nor Sioux. So she was following a hunch and going starboard.

The man had turned to partway face her, but nothing fine was showing in the black of an eye.

"Furry traders," she said.

"Not here," the man said.

"Not even Chippewa," the widow said. "Dunked." But it was harder than not by now to hear him. Did he say rock? Did he say just? Did he say paddle to port? Did she know where she was going, did he say? The widow felt a hewing up beneath her and through her, a succumbing coming up, and the heat of something not completely fathomed. "Father," she said.

Was she crazy? she heard. Rock, hull, she thought she heard, straight. But she was pressing through a history herself and said Marquette. They were not even Irish. Oh Joliet, she tried to say, oh Father—to hear how the sound of her voice was dissolving, melting, crazed. Fire-watered traitors, the widow tried to utter and could not—not quite. Shewano, Oconto, De Pere, the widow tried. Wauwatosa. Was he shouting, the man, at her? It seemed he was, for he was, after all, a man of his time, another time, another region. Was it Germantown? the widow tried to wonder. The city of Portage? Eau Claire? The

34

man's mouth was of the river, of the Peshtigo—the legend undertold. The widow's tongue tip tinned. Sheboygan, Superior, the widow tried to say as something in her sight began to cant. She was tilting to an unsung place—to a Peshtigoan dairyland delivered up to flame, a leak of history, a snuffing. O'Leary—this coincidence of consequential loss—Oh Prairie du Chien, she might have whispered. Did Chicago burn as willingly, as well? The widow was rushing through a sibilance of grace, through winded cities—bitter red, ash, bitter, bitter river, bitter shore. She was flicking off retention. Was there fire in the unblooded web of flesh and loin, a bone of knowing? Was there wedding of the elements? Did bottom-living minerals anneal?

This is second-guessing.

For a time, the empty boat would be a telling in itself, the man another christened vessel. And the widow? Oh widow—she would not not be counted. She would get to there, if only by the broken skin of dreams. For she'd conceived a destination such as this—to be found, to be found not wanting in the current, in the peril, in the rapture of a stream.

THE

TRICK

"RINSE it," said the woman whose guest she was, whose house this was, whose clothes she wore. "My advice," the woman said, "no salve."

The woman's name was Vera, and some last name—the consonants queerly resistant to tongue and to teeth.

"Awful," Vera said.

"Greasy," Vera said.

"Rita," Vera said, "I honestly wouldn't."

The faucet was on; the water was coming out hard. What Vera was telling her not to do—"No really, listen, Rita not"—was difficult for her to tell. The water made the wound look more pronounced. Not pink, not red, not even scarlet, no color Rita knew of.

"As if," Vera said, "you were trying to do yourself in."

Rita blotted herself with a cloth belonging to Vera, to Vera's spotless kitchen.

Something was pulsing.

"What is it?" Rita said.

"Whatever they've got on," Vera said. "Some band of his on tape."

It sounded aggressive.

"Turn it down, please," Vera said.

The men were fixing drinks. They were crouching, squatting, improving the position of the logs.

The men were laying odds.

"Lower," Vera said. "Down."

"What's that I smell?" one of the men, one of the husbands—Rita's—said. The husband's name was Dolan.

Dinner was casual, all in one pot. Ladled out. Con carne, Vera said. Delicious, Dolan said. Sweet, Rita said. There was custard in long-stemmed glasses, suited, it seemed to Rita, for something else.

Vera's husband spoke. His voice was unexpected for someone of his size. "Kindling," he said. "That is the honest-to-goodness difference."

"More?" Vera said, kept saying all during dinner. "Who wants more?"

"Turn that tape there," Dolan said.

The day had made them famished, or so they had concurred.

"Look at that wrist," Vera said. "Poor dear."

Rita looked at her spoon, at the mound of vanilla. She opened her mouth.

"Tomorrow," Dolan said, "just grab the thing. Don't think about it moving."

"The trick is not to think," Vera said.

Vera's husband reported a prediction, which had to do with weather.

"Will it?" Dolan said.

Vera said, "It's not supposed to stick."

Rita swallowed the custard, washed it down. Vera's

woolly pullover felt damp on Rita's body, rearranged (the women, in fact, were unalike in their proportions). "Maybe a little," Rita said. She lifted her tumbler. "Maybe a drop," she said. "Maybe a little, one drop more."

Vera brought a finger to the coil of her hair. A strand came loose. Her forearm seemed quite pale in the light of the fire. What she said was, "Sorry, love."

"NICE try," he said.

"Which?" she said.

They were somewhere other than under the quilt. She was moving to the bureau. It was one of those bureaus with a runner—oak, old solid oak; a person could rap it with a knuckle and know the way it was, and on it, all along the runner, which was certainly lace, there were feminine necessities: pins and lotions, scissors, a genuine boar bristle brush, a vial, a bottle with a V.

"Watch out," he said.

"I'm prone," she said.

His hands raised. "Look at you," he said. "Will you look at you?" he said.

There were paintings of nature, of natural scenery, in oil and in water on the walls.

"Smell," she said. "What do you think she keeps in here?"

They were thick, his hands.

"Don't," she said. She freed her wrist.

"Don't hurt yourself," he said.

• • •

THE house was of a definite type, quite common in the region: cream outside, off-white, with dark wood trim—chocolate, Vera called it, a house you could eat, styled as if it was on another continent. Out in the front was an empty brook, and past the empty brook, a slope. The slope was clear of trees. On fine cold days, there was, from the house's frontside windows, visible wintry action: the hint of a cap, bright, swift, the fluent suggestion of limbs—a leg's bend, an arm's crook—all headlong locomotion.

Inside was warm. No draft blew in. The bird in the clock plucked the accurate time. Nothing creaked. The house, despite appearances, was not, in fact, old—Vera had ordered it built. The plumbing was a dream, she said. The paint was new. The walls were new, and thin as injured skin.

"RISE and shine," Vera said. "Up and at 'em," Vera said, or something that sounded to Rita like that, to that effect. Everybody already was well up. Predictable scrubbings and flushings had occurred, as Rita was aware.

Rita had troubled with her eyes, with the shape and the blush of her lips, the general set of her face.

There was an odor of fried cured meat.

The men were in the nook.

"Sit," Vera said from somewhere in the kitchen.

Rita took a place.

"Really, I don't need help," Vera said.

The men had been betting on what sounded to Rita like a sporting event. Dolan hit the table. "You," he said. "You'll eat those words."

The shades had been lifted, and the day appeared fair. There were people on the slope.

Rita wore pants, and Vera, entering the nook, did too; the men did, too.

"Who wants what?" Vera said. She was holding a piled-high platter.

"I do," Dolan said.

"I'm good," said Vera's husband.

Rita doubled over a part of a sleeve, which was not the right fit.

"Wrong answer," Vera said.

"It isn't getting better," Rita said.

"Here, let me see," Vera said. She had put down the platter and was holding Rita's wrist to the light.

"I would say worse," Rita said.

Vera's husband was facing the window. "Powder," he said. It seemed that he had something in his mouth. "As I suspected," he said.

"Definitely worse," Rita said. "Is there anything at all in the house that I can use?"

Vera's husband was starting to clean Rita's plate—what was left, what she had not touched. The plates were rimmed around with maroon.

"Leave it alone," Vera said. "Don't pick."

Equipment was discussed—skis, poles, snacks.

"This color," Rita said.

Vera sniffed.

Somebody handed Rita a parka.

"Do we wear the same scent?" Vera said.

The men were yanking boots over socks.

"You're going to try it again," Dolan said. "Just do as I said. Just grab the rope."

"For God's sake," Vera said.

"I would say yes," Rita said. "The same."

Vera's husband adjusted a cap. "Isn't that what they say?" he said. "What's the expression? Back on the horse?"

Rita was looking at Vera, who looked to be examining the clamor of parquet.

"Isn't that what they say about what?" Rita said. "And what about it?"

TALL skis leaned against the house, tips crossed, poles slung by straps. Ice-rimed boots stood dripping by the door. The door was locked. There were glasses—stemmed, drained, or holding a hint of reddish liquid, drying, going sour in the nook. A glaze was on the window. The window was dark, the shades left carelessly up. Wraps were pegged haphazardly: parkas with thick down mitts stuffed down to rest in sleeves, fat hoods that left the side view blind. A tape had reached its end on the deck. In the grate, twigs sighed. Orchids imported from somewhere drooped. There was a leak in the sink, a clutter of dishes; a trail of thermal socks lay in the hall. The den was shut. A quilt was on the rug at the foot of the bed in the bedroom, night things, day things, soiled pairs of pants.

The mark—of the sort an open sore would leave on sheets—was scarcely perceptible.

Rita was angled on an arm. "Where are you?" she said.

The bird in the clock came out. Rita heard a masculine voice, what she took to be masculine speech. "Here," she said.

She rose, walked, opened a door.

A name was called.

A weak light fell.

Rita felt a sound fly out of herself. She touched herself, the base of her neck.

Pale at the end of the hall, arms seemingly boneless, the body a smear of flesh and chiffon, Vera appeared. "Dolan?" she said.

Rita wet her lips.

"Who is it?" Vera said. "Which one of the three of you is it?"

"WHAT did you think you were doing?" he said.

"Parched," she said.

"Parched?" he said.

Rita took a sip.

"Be decent," he said. "It's the middle of the night."

Rita put the sweaty-feeling glass on the unprotected table by the side of the bed. "How did I do today?" she asked. She leaned against the board, carved oak.

"You will notice I'm alive," she said.

There was noise in the hall, a deep cut of light beneath the door.

"The trick," she said, "is what again? Refresh me, please."

"Remember this: She was good enough to lend you her bed," he said.

"Stay put," he said.

Rita was stepping on her—or someone's—thrown-off clothes. The rug was bunched. Nob, edge, bristly surface, fingers to the bureau top; things revealed themselves by touch: cold throat of a vial, head of a pin, the absences made plain by implication. Lace—what felt to her like lace—was at her wrist.

Words were said. One of them might have been *dear.*

"What are they saying?" Rita said.

"Sleep," he said.

"His as well as hers," she said.

"Theirs," she said. "Their bed."

"The trick is 'go to sleep,' " he said.

"Dolan?" she said.

His head was on the pillow, as best she could tell.

"Where were you?" she said. She fingered something hard. "Where are you?"

"You would think you would know," he said, "that you gave her a scare."

Rita identified blades, as of quality scissors, snappable. "Dear," she said, "who's scared?"

BREAKFAST was boiled: coffee, oats—the latter congealing in the last clean pot. Every utensil was crusted, mealy. Dolan had gone. Vera had gone along in the car, her car. They had gone to get eggs, milk, gauze.

"Cowboy," Vera's husband said. He raised his cup.

Rita blew over the rim of hers.

"Do you know what I mean?" he said.

"Strong," he said.

"I'm not in the mood to talk," she said. "Turn some music on."

He drank.

"So tell me, then," she said. "Do you know what they're doing? Say it."

"They've gone to get more food," he said. "Victuals. And something for the wrist."

"Provisions," she said.

"Fog," he said. The slope appeared empty.

"Awful," she said.

"For now," he said. Meat, sweat, curdling cream, a soupy, florid perfume—the house stank of everything in it. "Rita," he said, "do you know what it is that Vera says is awful?"

Rita turned a cuff. "This?" she said.

"Whose shirt do you have on?" he said.

"It's hers," she said.

"Mine," he said.

"When did they say they'd be back?" she said.

"Who knows?" he said. "More?"

She touched her wrist. It oozed.

"Please," she said. "More hot."

He led her to the sink in the kitchen. Overfilled. The counters overtaken.

Her hands were on a sponge, a dish, a bowl.

"Leave it be," he said.

"I can't," she said. "Can I?"

Sock against sock on the way to the bathroom.

Blush was in the sink—great, violent smudges of feminine color.

The faucet had power.

"Piping," he said.

A steam came up.

"Okay?" he said.

His face was near to hers, sinewed, damp, a foreign expression in the eyes. "Say it," he said. "Do you know what I want?"

"Not this," she said.

"Clearly not this," she said.

He let his breath out thickly. His breath smelled of her.

"Infected," she said.

A slam seemed to come from the house's entry.

"You," she said. She held his wrist.

"No, you," he said. "Why can't you even call me by my God-given name?"

SHE flushed: cream, pins—safety and bobby—gel and balm, lace she had spoiled discreetly in the night. It was exactly as Vera had said: a reverie of flushing. Pungent. Rita rubbed her eyes. She tossed down the last of the fluid in a bottle, wiped her reddened mouth. She closed the jars, replaced them, empty, on top of the bureau: Nothing would seem amiss at a glance.

She opened things, slitted things.

"What took so long?" she said.

Stride, sweat, height—it was Dolan in the door frame, Dolan in the room.

She was holding a brush as if looking for hairs.

He took it right out of her hand. "That husband of Vera's," he said.

"He knows," she said.

"What do you think he knows?" he said.

A painting—an oil—looked crooked on the wall.

"Why don't you lower your voice?" she said.

"Too late," he said. "Who are you really jealous of?"

Her back was to the bed.

"Did I warn you?" he said. "Don't say I never did."

THERE should have been some kind of scenic relief: snow, wind, hail, a bloody commotion on the slope. But it was nightfall again. There were only the people in the house— the gaping brook, the treeless runs, the localest of elements were too removed to be of any consequence to them.

Parquet was at their legs. They sat there, chairless, eating with their fingers out of cartons. A vase had been felled. A bird had flown into the window, snapping its neck, but this was not evident, dark as it was. Wads of gauze were strewn about.

"This is what you wanted," Vera said. "I believe."

"Is it?" Rita said.

"What is it you believe?" Vera's husband said to Rita.

Dolan said, "Salt."

Vera's husband was licking his fingers. "Taste and smell," he said. "The same. One is like the other."

Rita was using a hand, an arm. Sauce was on her skin.

"Do I owe you?" Dolan said.

The coil of Vera's hair had come undone.

"How much is the damage?" Dolan said.

Vera's husband said, "Plenty."

"For what?" Vera said. "The food? The tow? That awful, awful incident?"

Rita filled her mouth.

There was a spitting in the grate.

Vera's husband said, "A wager is a wager."

"A what?" Rita said. "A what is a what?"

"Right," Dolan said.

Vera set a carton of rice on a square of the floor. "Translate," she said.

Rita was looking at Dolan. She tore off a festering gauze. "Translation," she said.

Vera said, "Stop. Just stop."

Dolan took his wallet out. "Get alcohol," he said.

so they brought out the sheets.

There were duties to attend to, involving the ashes, sinks, the bed; there were chores with which a guest was expected to help. The house was of a type, after all, that was not meant for living.

The women had done what they could with rags.

The men were hauling gear; they were tying the skis to the racks with rope.

It was the women who would be the last to leave. "A form of protection," Vera said: sheet by sheet, room by room, every stick of furniture, Vera at an end and Rita at another—fresh, these sheets. Oak went white. Things would be tidy, Vera said; and quiet, Rita said, and dry— as if pristine, as if, in fact, untouched.

TABLE

TALK

SHE is every place there is inside my house. She is here inside the cases with the books and files and records; she is rattling in the cupboards with the saucers and the cups. She is in the window sashes. She is dripping from the faucets; she is creaking in the hinges; she is matted in the brushes, tooth and fingernail and hair. She is in the dresser drawer with the bras and socks and underpants, the panty hose, the pills. She is blowing through the radiators, waiting in the hamper, frosting up the Frigidaire. She is in my husband's closet with the ties and the trousers. She is in between the sheets and on the pillows, breathing breath.

I NEVER answer the phone.

WHEN my sister sends a letter, I save the envelope.

· · ·

SHE is sitting at my kitchen table taking soup.

I say, "A little table talk." I say, "What happened to your hair?"

She says, "Just look why don't you maybe at what happened to my wrist."

I say, "You'd better see a dentist."

She says, "Mother loved you better."

I say, "Have another napkin. Have a sponge."

She says, "The times I saved your neck."

She says, "The husband and the house."

She says, "You don't have any biscuits left. I looked."

ACTUALLY, my sister has never had soup at my kitchen table. I will not allow soup in my house.

I NEVER seem to have postage.

SHE is in the argument I'm having with my husband where I bang the drawers and run the tap and rattle forks and knives and dishes piled in the sink.

He says, "Try opening your ears."

He says, "Besides and furthermore."

He says, "In fact, in fact, in fact."

WE keep an extra box of biscuits in each and every cupboard—just in case.

· · ·

SHE is in my address book inside my bedside table. She is listed under *s* in all the spaces. She is listed under *t* and *u* to catch the overflow, and when I dial wrong old numbers on the Touch-Tone, she still answers anyway.

I AM afraid of dirty dishes, empty boxes, paper wrappers, bread crumbs, termites, leaks, and stains.

ALSO crackers.

MY sister's latest letter says that she has dyed her hair.

EACH week I shine the woodwork, polish doorknobs, open windows, vacuum carpets, beat the rugs. I pack up boxes full of books and cheese and dry goods that I have around the house and seal the boxes tight with tape, and I see to it that my husband bleeds the radiators clean.

HE says, "Go answer it yourself."

I WASH down contraceptive pills.

. . .

SHE is in the water glass. She is in the bathroom sink. She is in the toothpaste tube. She has my nose.

WE are always low on bleach.

SHE says, "Who can see your face across a telephone long distance?"

She says, "Can't you come and see me?"

I say, "Glad to hear that you received the scarf."

She says, "I've got a sofa here."

She says, "I'll let you have the bed."

She says, "I loved you like a mother would and would you even recognize my face?"

I say, "The wash is in the dryer." I say, "Something's in the oven." I say, "All the floors need wax." I say, "The fridge is on the blink." I say, "The thermostat just broke." I say, "The tub is overflowing." I say, "You must see I cannot leave my house in this condition when you know that I am here and all alone, all by myself."

SEEDS

IN

PUBLIC

PLACES

WHAT my mother is saying to me about pearls is that you must rub them against your teeth. "Like this," my mother is saying to me, demonstrating, moving an earring over her lowers. "Friction."

I am engaged to be married. The shoes are flat. The dress needs something else, my mother says, some accessory or accent. The veil could stand a press.

We are in my mother's master bedroom, where we are looking in my mother's box of jewels; at least, that is where I have been looking. Sun is coming through the windowpanes, showing up motes.

It is dazzling.

I have sometimes seen men turn and watch my mother as she's walking on the sidewalk. I believe this happens often.

My mother says that she has always followed certain necessary rules, which she has tried to teach to me: Break your rolls; powder your feet; don't eat foods with seeds in public places.

I love the things that sparkle in this box my mother has. I love the box, which is lined with ruby velvet.

"It's a trick," my mother says, "which a woman ought to know." My mother puts the earring back. I see her lipstick on it. "If there isn't grit, it's paste," she says.

"If things we owned could talk," my mother said to me last week as she was teaching me to recognize the sound of fine crystal.

I watch my mother fiddle with a clasp. "These are real," my mother says, and holds the strand against my throat. "See? See how delicate? How right?"

But I am trying to pick out something shiny.

"Look," I tell my mother. "I think the dress wants something else."

"Listen here," my mother says to me. "Trust me."

I have my finger on a ring I used to notice on my mother's slender hand. It is opal. "Go ahead," my mother says. "It's yours."

My mother has told me not to mix gold with silver.

"They are knotted in between," my mother is telling me. "They can be restrung," she says. "See the subtle luster?"

She says, "Really, you should give a thing a chance."

"Just this once," my mother says.

"Never mind," my mother says to me. "Forget I mentioned anything." She starts to ball the pearls up in her palm, and this action makes a noise.

"Mama?" I say.

"What now?" my mother says.

THE

SEER

IT looked at first to be an office of some sort, dimly, even sleepily, lit. To look at it, she thought, what with the windows of it gated, what with the door of it secured, you would have thought it deserted.

She checked the address. She checked the address again. This was not an office district. That the number on the door was the same as the one on the dampened scrap—the blurred scrawl the signature of Mr. Edward's fountain pen and less than reliable, these days, grip—well!—it didn't serve to reassure her, did not, as she would doubtless have said had she had a companion, inspire in her confidence or faith. This whole block! Its shotgun houses scattershot, slatted and weedy, a stronghold, it seemed, of vacant lots, not a body in a yard, the sense of insects pervasive.

Often, as now, she shaped her thoughts as if for someone else.

She knew she did.

She knocked, of course. Of course, she touched her

hair, a habit she had failed, somewhere along the way, to lose. It was not for lack of not quite effort but urging. Under a hat, her face, still good, she thought, if not quite young, partook of shade. Her pocketbook, embattled leather warrior, was guarding a hip.

There was a bell to the side of the door. She found it—the bell, the buzzer. Whatever it was, it was mounted in tin, and was crooked as the step on which she stood. She rang or buzzed—either. She would say to Mr. Edward—what would she say? Composing, composing herself. That who should answer but dogs, or dog? She tended to exaggerate. The barking and the scratching, however, were real, the sound of dogs' paws, of the nails of the paws of a carnivorous animal on wood.

The door swung in. A nose poked out. A long-legged man appeared in the doorframe. To see them both, the man, the dog, graying and angular, sniffing, you might as well think it true, what was said about the looking-alike, attraction or living the means to it.

"Good morning," she said, though it was, in fact, later than this.

The man just stood, he with his shirt a fright, the tails of it tortured. The face bespoke illness, why else to be creased and flushed this way, or maybe of only a recent, likely fully-dressed inebriated nap.

"Come in," the man said.

And so she did. It was almost as if she could see herself. With a hand to the hair, to the hat, to the battered pocketbook—still and all tasteful—here she was: She was a woman with a mission, a woman with a scarcely perceptible limp, as if merely a slightly lazy stride (persuaded thus, she soldiered on). She was a woman with a scrap to the dog.

The dog began to circle.

"Do you know who I am?" she said, and, stepping back, "Does that dog bite?"

It was scarcely lazy.

"No," the man said. "Sit. I said sit."

There was nowhere a chair. There was a lingering gloom, promoted, she thought, by smell: disinfectant and dog and a masculine essence and something else familiar that she could not identify, nevertheless. What appeared to be a medical examining table, covered unhygienically, she'd had to have added, had anyone asked, the wrinkled paper seeming much the worse for what she'd had to have said had been multiple uses—this table, this was the point, for there was no time to waste, for she was here about business, personal in nature though it was, point being it was out in plain sight. There was nothing like a stethoscope, nothing like a needle or gauze. There was no framed medical diploma. There was, she saw, stacked, a supply of dispensable towels, coarse, such as might be dispensed near a sink in a not-so-gentle, public, even flea-ridden, place.

It was, anyway, the dog who sat. It was the dog who sat, and whined, and seemed eager, ready, poised to jump—a silver-nosed projectile. Make no mistake: What there was in the eyes was a roiling sense of injustice, at war with appeal to the master for release.

"Sit," the man said.

Defeat, humiliation. In the eyes of the dog, in the dream of the eye, a life bereft of hope.

It was not without rage.

"The dog," she said. And on seeing the man did not see the question, "What do you call the dog?" she said, this creature in an anguish of malevolent restraint. If there was something she had learned, it was this: Familiarity or friendship, or maybe it was knowledge, could vanquish all. She had had an education. "To what does he answer to?" she said.

"Penny," the man said.

"Penny?" she said. "Penelope?"

The man did not repeat it. He patted himself on the front of the shirt as if seeking tobacco, change, or some flawed comfort pocketed in haste.

That the dog was a female, to think of it—Penny! Gray Penny—why, she had to admit, it altered the way the dog looked. She had clung to assumption, had she not, adhered to an idea of a rabid masculinity (a cat being female).

The obvious made obvious—"Penny," she said.

So called, the dog, Penny, arose, an obvious and tawdry nuzzler of knees, of dress, of dangled pocketbook.

Eyeballed, the master shrugged.

"Mrs.—Ida," she said, unclasping, clasping. Buried within, amid the billfold, pills, a brush, pressed powder in a compact, deep inside in her pocketbook, her scrap, damply rumpled, a secret re-concealed, was laid uneasily to rest. She had nothing to offer the dog at all. So as not to be sidetracked (how had it taken all this while, her whole life, it seemed, with its paid education, its civic tour of duty, and so forth, its beige corrective shoes, for her to get to where she was?), so as not to be distracted, she spoke of

Mr. Edward, invoking his health. That such a man such as he should have to suffer—

"Rex," the host said, hand held gauntly out to her, and yellow-nailed. Of jaundiced manners, nonetheless the looming and undeniable host: Did she maybe require a beverage? he said.

"Me?" she said. Thinking, could she take that hand?

"Yourself," Rex said. "The one and the same." For it was not for Mr. Edward, he said, he suspected, that she, Ida, honestly had come to here to him—"now, Ida, now have you?"—and wasn't she here on behalf of herself? He could recognize the look, the hesitant gait. "You have suffered a loss," Rex said.

No, she would not take that hand. Her face, she feared, was moist, a telltale sheen about the nose. Applied frugally, her powder had surely been absorbed. It was hot. The hat itched. She had drool on her stockings. "Penny," she said to no discernible result.

"Penelope," she said to hot breath on the shin.

The hand still waited.

"Water," she said. She would relish a cold glass of water with cold crushed ice.

"Can't do," Rex said. "The water isn't drinkable."

"Goodness," she said, and then, "You're wrong." She heard herself, took note of herself, feeling, then seeing the slatted day darken through a window, midday gone. The hour entered the bloodstream. Pure wrought iron. "I am here on a promise," she said. "I am keeping my promise, true to my word. That's all."

With this, the hand withdrew itself.

Penny affected a nothing less than hangdog expression.

She, Ida, flinched. "Mr. Edward," she said, her rather enfeebled, yet, of course, still deeply respected employer, of mutual acquaintance, she presumed, had sent her, insisted, in fact, that the matter was entirely utmost. She was loyal to a fault, she had to admit. She said, "He said you'd know."

"I know. You have suffered a loss," Rex said as he apparently followed and somehow invaded her gaze. It fell to the examining table. "Look at me," he said. "Do you know your eyes are red?"

She touched her eyelids—one and the other, in an almost involuntary, foolish, she might have conceded, gesture, as if with the faith that a person could finger a redness there, could identify a color or shade through skin, as if the senses had been thoroughly denied their limitations. She fingered moisture. Dismayed, she tried again, confirmed it: Pink, at least, as if fear of the thing was the thing that had made it so. This and the man's presumption. "The air," she said. "The air," and thought, dust— dust and worse. Motes, she thought, and here she was, a swollen-ankled woman with a compromised mien. She was hugging, even choking, her pocketbook; would that she were in it, inside it, she and her sundries, she and her necessities, she and her scrap. If only she were hidden in the bowels of the thing! But here she was, alone in a room with a need and the voice in her head; a man, of course, certainly, a man, of course, and rather less expectedly, rather more pointedly, a dog, a carrier, heaven knew of what, and she herself, Ida, with a delicate system, thirsty and worn, her forearms moist on poreless leather, pock-marked; the irritant spores—was it spores?—the word that inserted itself in her thoughts; it was a general invisible itch.

Rex smiled.

Just smiled yellowly, the gaps in abundance, while Penny continued to conspicuously breathe.

"What are you?" Ida said, attempting—she wouldn't have argued, had anyone asked—in this way to regain herself. "Are you some kind of doctor? Some kind of medical doctor?"

"Do I look like a medical doctor?" he said.

She smelled decay.

"No," she said. "You look, shall I say it, unwell, or, if you don't mind my saying it, indisposed, in the spirit in which it is meant, of course."

"Of course," Rex said.

"I mean," she said, "that is—Penny, Penelope, please," she said. "Desist." Forbearance was in order. She needed refreshing. The towels, as previously noted, were stacked; there was a look of spit and rub about the host, this Rex.

She had prided herself on her sensitive skin: "Look at this rash," she would say as if saying, see my ring, do take care with the china, lifting her chin to a minimal light.

Damp palms on dress, not a hint of relief in the offing—"Is there nowhere," she said, "where a person can possibly sit?"

Rex answered by way of a sideways nod: The table, take it or leave it, the nod seemed to say.

"Are you, you mustn't be serious, are you?" she said.

"That is to say, in earnest," she said.

"Oh," she said. "Oh, dear."

There was a look of wanton shedding and worse about the dog.

Given a moral interest, even more than a moral interest in this, Ida made up her mind: She would tell Mr. Edward, as soon as she saw Mr. Edward again, or soon enough, or in due course—dear sweet man, to think of it!—she would say she had thought that she would not, that she would never, at least in this lifetime, believe her, do what she had done, or rather, was about to do, she with her special-ordered soap (twice daily bather!), she with her conditions, yet do it she did. She sat with a crinkle.

The glass was in her hand.

"Your loss," Rex said.

Wrung towel of the sort to be found in an ill-washed restroom in whatever rest stop or station of transit, a bane to the skin; it was tight in her opposite fist. "Mister," she said, to a *shhh.*

"Mister Edward," she said.

"Yourself," Rex said, as he had said, it seemed to her before—herself indeed! She heard a newfound element of coaxing in the tone of the voice. "Ida," he said, "the part you remember."

"The part I remember of what?" she said—her selfsame self indeed! He meant for her to offer it, doubtless. What came to her (eyes closed, feet up, for they were, after all, swollen and she was not young, not quite, and had she not traveled considerable distance? And evening was on her, ambiguous balm, and here he was, her reckless host, slurring encouragements, and here was Penny breathing, Penelope breathing, breathing, and here she was, Ida, in spite of herself, verbosely limping Ida, methodical Ida; she knew how she was seen, for she was not unintelligent, not unaware, not a bit: She had a putative gift of perception, or so she had heard, or anyway had overheard, or at the least had told herself), what came to her all but unbidden was this: a surface, a morsel of a life, her life. There were floors she had learned with hands and knees, by heart, by skin—the issue of servants; intransigent bones of the body at its work. The rooms she had moved through! Chairs she had dusted with only her fingers, scavenged whiffs of scent: soap, wood, drains, fear (where was it she had put that glass? and had it not pearled?), a scent of a delectable decay; why, it went, did it not, with the slowing over time of an asymmetric pace, of a motion in the world, the parts she had inhabited, barbiturate of dutiful living. She could almost picture the voice in her head, in her ear: You have suffered a loss, you have suffered an injury, Ida, Ida. What was there of this? She could see, if she tried (she did, did try), she could see Mr. Edward's musty desk—the lamp shade green, the blotter green—and there at the woolly knee of him, a girl. There were ribbons she had worn, a dress she had sewn, a doleful hat: black with net with black dots in front of her forehead, an elegant obstruction, herself a proper orphan, funereal child, and after, the force she could feel of an arm, the black, black hair of an arm, sweaty and vivid as invention. Well, perhaps she had invented it, a practical woman, something from nothing. A hiccup of the mind: You have suffered an injury, Ida, Ida.

Her body at an angle from the wrong-angled leg, a weed in the hand, her hair. "Blood from a turnip," she said.

"Drink," the voice said.

She had been urged not to touch it. Her hand had been licked. Her pocketbook lay in a sprawl at the edge of her thoughts. Crickets in the field where she lay. A hand to the hair. A full-bodied fluid in the mouth. Ida, oh, Ida. The name rang wrong in the ear.

"Does the name ring wrong in the ear?" Rex—for it was certainly Rex—seemed to purr.

"Wrong?" she said. Outside here were weeds, she knew, and vines, and there were rotted-out slats, and doors half out of their rotted-out hinges, and ravening creatures of the ravening night. "Wrong?" she said. "What is it that you've done? Do you call it a skill, this thing, whatever it is? Do you call it a gift? Is it some kind of evil gift?"

Her eyes were half-open. Her clothes, it seemed to her, had been completely disarranged. "Were it not for Mr. Edward . . ." she said.

"Then what?" Rex said.

"Don't try me," Ida said. Her cheeks felt newly and familiarly rashy. Hives, she thought. She would tell Mr. Edward, if ever she saw Mr. Edward again (to think of it distressed her, but was he not, in fact, quite frail, quite terribly frail? She could scarcely assemble specifics of the face, the stance. The nose, she thought, was it not bent ever so slightly, as if it had been broken; the forehead, as she had told herself, in phrases she had written in her mind and had taken dearly to heart, had saved as if for speech, for an appropriately elevated discourse, and not for such a man such as Rex to presume to read into her inmost thoughts, was it ever so high? How well had he held the pen in his hand?), she would tell Mr. Edward . . . what? That she had been robbed? That she had got lost? Had lost her way? It was, after all, a scrap, potentially illegible.

The hand was less than steady.

Penny, she saw, had got hold of the hat, small measure of shade, and was gnawing, with violent patience, the rim.

"I am not quite well," said Ida. "Listen to me."

"Not well," said Rex. "And nor am I."

The sight of it! Straw after straw in the mouth. She could scarcely remember the look of the hat or the feel of the hat on herself. Her face would not come back to her. Towel to the hairline—"Please . . ." she said. "Mr. Edward . . ." she said. "Our mutual acquaintance . . ." she said. "Why, I promised. . . ." she said.

Her pocketbook lay open and empty, she saw, a gaping, a leathery and tongueless, mouth.

There was nothing of hers.

No personal effect.

Not a scrap.

"Mr. Edward is gone," Rex said.

"Gone?" she said.

The dog had moved on to the ribbon of the hat.

"Gone," Rex said, "passed out of this life."

Through no known office of body or mind, she saw that this was so, saw the man, Mr. Edward, standing before her, leaked ink wounding the front of the shirt; he was yellowly breathing, and gone.

The hand held out was sallower than ever before.

Ida stood and took a step. She limped. She had not lost her limp.

The dog's cheeks bulged.

The dog's eyes brightened.

"Penny," said Ida, and lowered herself to get hold of a shoe, to get hold of a lace, to untie the thing. "Penelope," she said, "come here—come on."

SOMEWHERE

NEAR

SEA

LEVEL

HERE is my father. He is tucking in a tongue. Coaxing. Lacing, doubling a knot. My ankles are weak. The rink is lit. My father's hands are darkly livered, veined. Use, he says, has done this.

"Can you stand?" my father says.

The ice, I see, is swept, wet, white. "Try standing," my father says. "Up." There is forcefully dampered music, piped. There is no sky. No rain, no threat. "See it?" my father says. "Look." No hint. It used to be something else, this forceful place. "Before your time," he says.

He looks like my father.

"Gone," he says.

"Dad?" I say. I am gaining my feet. There is something, I think, or nothing, hairline, cleft.

Deep. The voice. "Steady."

A person could be dizzy.

"You almost can see it."

"Dad?" I say.

It is dizzying.

"Things I could tell you," my father is telling me. He is inflection, timbre; unfamiliar and expected in the far-away, fatherly way he always has. "Gloves . . ." he says. "Folds . . ." I feel the after-rills of phrases, words between the words I am invariably failing to catch. "A curtain there . . . an arch . . ."

A ramp's slope.

What I want is to skate. I do. Want to. Want and want to want. Pulsing my toes, my fingers restless, ragged-nailed. "Now?" I say.

My father is talking marble and Saturday. "Nights," he says, whatever, I don't know. "Glass," he says, or "Hats," he says.

"Tails," he says.

"These skates," I say. "My toes."

My father is pressing for fit, says, "Gutted." I feel it. "Better?" he says.

I have had practice.

"Better," I say. "Better, please." My ankles flinch.

There is a woman in the middle of the middle of the ice, going backward. Curve and grace is what she is, and speed, and speed.

There is knowing in the body. My father is touching my elbow, glancingly, knowingly, fluidly moving beside me, before me, ushering me from behind.

"The center is lower," my father says, "in a girl."

The woman appears to me to be weightless.

"Why?" I say. "What center?"

"Didn't I tell you?" my father says.

She is all lift.

I am in a wobble.

"Never mind," my father says.

I am making my father fall, almost. I almost could.

"Easy, easy does it," my father says. "Use your head, for heaven's sake."

I am flailing for his arm. "Tell me," I say. "Now." My father is smartly just past reach. "Why?" I say.

"You know," he says, "a person can not hear you."

Habit. Fearborne. Sleeves, snaps, cuffs. I am speaking to a bead, to a fearful pearlish glinting in myself. "This place," I say, "was what?"

"Careful," my father says.

There is a ceiling, of course. Always was. Flight's worth up. It burns, the ice, rebukes my back. Flat flung limbs. Nothing is broken, my father says. Birds, I say. It is terribly high, even given style, even given flights, even given tricks with scarves. A person could stand on a person's shoulders, given even balance, a bent for stunt, feint—a lady fluttering, swooning, waft and lilt and pale, light, sweet perfume, airily, deftly arcing off a balcony—taken down, removed.

My father is furrow and how many fingers.

"Who?" I say.

"Who do I look like? Please," I say.

"My name?" I say.

"What day?" I say.

"Wait," I say. "My ankle," I say, "hurts." It all comes

back—oh, the power of the powerfully helpless. "Hurts,"
I say.

"Let me," my father says. "Will you?"

"WON'T," I say. "Will not," I say, "help." This is only a
portion of an answer in advance.

Now you see it: My father's skates are scarred, if from
daring or storage, I do not know—in houses, cellars,
wrecked and vaulted rooms, strewn, or bound, paired,
dolled in attic rags, sleeves, yokes, the ruined drapes, the
molded sheets—in plundered trunks, a chest; a lavish ef-
flux: See under spawn and brackish fissure, over sunken
seams, ridge, reef; see under floe; see under yaw, in another
time zone, found.

By the way, I am married.

"Won't," I say, "help."

I am kneeling and fanning and lying.

I am not a child.

"Let me," my father says, "see it?"

I say, "Will you?"

I SAY, "Please," or I say, "Look," or "Hurts," I say. He is
touching my elbow, hair, my arm. We are in an aisle; he is
touching a veil, net, necklace—luminous, inherited; I am
carrying lilies; there is no breeze; I am carrying nothing,
blood; we are in rooms, in years, in the rending of an in-
stant, cleaving in the yawning dark, curled, here, gone. He
is touching a shoulder—blade, wing—nobbed, insistent

back. "What?" he says. "I can't," he says, "hear you, make sense of you, the way you turn away."

HE is holding my foot, my father is. "Flex," he says.

The woman jumps.

"How does it feel?" my father says.

"Sore," I say. Impossible, the height. . . .

"Very sore."

. . . The woman lilts, floats, rises, impossibly rises.

"Sprained," I say. (I have had lessons.) "Horribly sprained."

"Not likely," my father says. "Couldn't. You hardly were moving."

"Was," I say.

"Can't be," he says.

"Could," I say.

"Could so," I say.

"You are so small," my father says. "You didn't have very far to—"

"Wait," I say. "There was a second in the air, I remember, when everything—"

"Slipped," my father says. We are all interruption.

"Spun," I say. "It—"

"—Most you did was slip," my father says. "Scratched, tops. More or less—"

"Please," I say.

"More or less nothing." My father is moving. "I am waiting," he says.

"Still waiting," he says.

"Can't hear you," my father says.
I am on bony, graceless knees.
The woman is glowing, effulgent.
I could be imploring.

"TELL me," he says. "What?"

There is a way that whatever you turn away from owns your heart. There is a way that it doesn't.

He is touching my neck, a clasp, mesh. We are under a shimmering sky.

He is still waiting.

I am in white. "Carry me," I say.

NIGHTJARS

FROM there, they went north. Not due north, but north. What difference? Fearless, or nervy with fear, young—she younger than he was, unless she was lying. Cold, too. She was cold, she said. He turned cuffs. No coat. No heels. Deliberate earth. "I am never cold," he said. He unbuttoned. Rude streets. The sorrow of commerce in a town passed through. A qualmy, lonely light. It was always a certain kind of day in the places where they were not expected. Broken. "Salt," she said. She liked to lurk, or said she did, or mostly did, or did not mind, she said. She was keen, she said, of certain necessary senses. Torsos, armless in windows, beckoned—faces planed and shopworn chins aloof. She registered keenly, slanted into arrogance. He inhaled. What she smelled was salt, she said, greasy and vended, and sweat-soaked flannel, and rusty, wasted cats. She predicted weather. Board, chalk, brick. Cashier. An alley, germy and wrappered, delinquently wet. She stole. He paid. They stole. Squares peeled off, gray as the rumbling vehicle gray of slow escape. She was hoarding unnatural heat. A city of cripples, tipped and caned, went tottering by. Planks and spires—nowhere for his knees, he said, on this poor bus; litter in the aisle—poles and lean-tos, shambling, water-rotted shacks with laundry drably flapping, a chicken in the dirt looking lost. "No?" she said. "Yes," he said, agreeing. He was tall in these parts. She chattered. Futile, this artificial heat. Nothing was growing. A vista gaped: grainy, reliefless, limbless nothing, corroded, expired, until the eyes renewed it. Their eyes did. Birds rose. Stiff fields cropped up. Trees sprawlingly rooted, restless, wormy flanks, a river veering gangly, passably north.

Go on.

Name her.

Rae will do.

It did for him.

He called her that, Rae. He went by Frank, and Hal, and Tom, Wayne, Wade, Enoch, and also, once, in a bygone place, by Juan. Need, he said. Need and latitude. Depending, he said. She could depend, Rae could, he said, on this, the need, whichever way it was he went—by land, by ditch, by various, sometimes-legal strategies, chap-lipped, largely loosely strung, unevenly featured, if fair. "Hans?" he said. "Lars?"

She called him Vern.

It got darker faster the farther north they went.

They went far.

There were scenes, of course, some quiet. Does it matter what was said? And who did not answer? And how it was that she, Rae, might have looked, in a setting, from an angle, in sleep? "Still," he said. "Too still," he said. A quiet prod. "I am sleeping," she said, turning—never a blanket, no pillow. "Not me," he said. "I never am sleeping. Rae?" he said. "Doll," he said, some other place. Her cheek on prayered hands, her hair, its darkness spilling in a dark arrangement as if in the wave of a dream.

There was something like a smile on her lips.

He smiled, nearly. What he did, it seemed, was watch.

"Mercy," she said. Awake in a changed landscape, saying it, *mercy,* or something like it, like a curse. Such fists she had—a child's. The eyes she was born with. A rub. "Where am I?" she said, was everywhere saying.

Bent. Trapped. A too-small and vastly horrible enclosure. The world inside her mouth. A roiling basin. Her wan face—flipped, a mole on the opposite cheek, the only way to see herself, reversed. Knocking. A clockwise rush, as was correct. A trickle in a drain.

Knocking.

Coffee from somewhere.

"Vern?" she said.

"Milk?" she said, not too much farther on.

"I could rightly eat," she said.

"You could?" he said.

"Could you?" she said.

"Could I?" he said.

Thick crepe soles. An aproned, creamy hip, belonging to a woman awaiting an order. A pencil, apparently gnawed.

"If wishes were gravy," Rae said.

"What then?" he said.

"We'd both be as big as a house," she said. She cupped a cup with ashy, slender fingers as if absorbing sustenance.

"We'll get there," he said.

"Will we?" she said. "Where is it, this house?"

She, it seemed, could scarcely sit.

"Vern?" she said.

"George," he said. "What was the question?"

Knives, stubs, crumbs, a map on a place mat, locks she'd picked, and pilfered, cut-rate condiments were barely concealed in dubious sites about her person. There was something in her bosom.

"What is it?" he said.

"We'll starve," she said.

"No," he said.

"You're right," she said. "Likely we'll freeze first."

Picture a low-slung man. Low-slung men slunk by. Eggs, meat, fat slung-out stacks of cakes. "Mercy, mercy me," she said. All belly, these eaters, and just about visibly silver-lined pockets—hip, front—and cloudy expressions and humid, insinuating posture.

"Not much of a question, is it?" he said. He rolled his sleeves, his gait. "Gents," he said.

She predicted travel.

"Myself and my wife," he said.

"Shove over," she said.

"Crook," she said. "I knew it."

His skin was bright. They were bumping in the bed of a truck. Distended tracks lay on the earth. Small stones were flying. "Rae?" he said. "How can a person sleep?" she said. Glazed, raw—a plaintively lovely vegetation. She tasted herself. This was not sex: vagrant, edgy union— theirs—conjoining in an alley, a pew, in the middle of some earthly nowhere, planted, lying, lying down. This was not that. "I am freezing," she said.

It snowed.

"Listen," she said. "Are you listening?" Thick snow lit

on her lashes. Her hair went slowly gray. Her face she held slantwise.

"Look at my hands," she said.

"Feel my hands," she said. "Ice."

His shirt was drenched. His back seemed somehow to vibrate, distinct from her, apart from the bump and grind of riding, herky-jerky, on too many threadbare wheels.

"I am burning up," he said, when what he was doing was seizing up.

A low moon slid.

Rae formed a syllable. Shook dark her hair. Blanketed him with the insubstantial wrap of her body, little of it as there was.

Gourds, a branch, a rootlike object—things showed warped, defying their rightful contours.

"Vern," she said.

"You," she said. "Are you listening, you?"

She sat. A stain defined her dress.

Something glinted.

"Quiet," she said. "Brother," she said. "This is the actual plan."

IT had a snout. Hair. A piggy-looking countenance. Sores traversed its sides and creepy insectile creatures were greedily rooting in its flesh. One of its eyes was gone, was nothing but a bloody, yawning aperture. It wouldn't have even half-wanted to look at itself—so compromised and disaligned, all tumor and gristle, a tumorous plug at its rear. It leaked. Trodden, spat-on, bled-on, lumpy, leaked-on and festering hay—or something similarly haylike—

was all that passed in this place for floor. Stuck on the walls, as if they had grown themselves, there were parts. Teeth. Gears. Implements bristled with rust. A trigger, a hammer.

Someone or something sneezed.

A flame gleamed faintly.

"Vern," Rae said.

He did not answer, save to moan.

"What *is* that piggy thing?" Rae said.

"What does it look like?" a woman, apparently tender of it, asked Rae. The woman's dress seemed wrongside out. Her gaze was moist. Her stockings were pouching at her ankles in a fallen condition.

"Whatever it is," Rae said, "it stinks."

The line in which they waited twitched, scratched—another rank thing, afflicted with its own supplication. Steaming on the exhale. Its end, or rather, its head, was a brittle-looking man, guiding, as best he could, a doubly brittle-looking needle. Obviously, he was old. His purchase was poor. The needle was bloody.

"Hold your tongue," the woman said.

Something brayed.

"There," the old man said. Trembled. Patted a lavishly vaccinated joint.

Rae angled toward the flame.

"Hold your place," the woman said, stroking her charge's snout.

The old man's hands were singed.

"Where?" Rae said. "Where am I?"

"Next," the old man said.

"That would be us," the woman said. "Doc?"

It wouldn't have wanted to look at even half of itself as singed hands poked, hazarded a thump.

"What do you reckon?" the woman said.

Out of the brittle lips, a word: "Deceased."

"No," the woman said.

"I reckon," he said.

"Vern?" Rae said. "Vern? Doc?"

"Some doc," the woman said. "This here is breathing."

The old man thumped again, slightly southward, provoking a high, corrosive squeal.

"See?" the woman said.

"Dead," he insisted. "Or equally good as."

Down off the wall came a bristly shotgun. "Stand back and duck," he said, taking awful aim.

Teeth clattered. Something pinged. A wind blew biting through a hole.

"Vern?" Rae said.

An ominous sound, possibly terminal.

"Stop," the woman said.

"Give it here," Rae said.

"Stop, you!" the woman said.

The floor began to rise in festering pieces as shot after shot missed its target.

"Give it," Rae said. She grabbed. Clenched. Squeezed.

A piggish expulsion hit the hay.

"Now look," the woman said.

"Doc," Rae said.

"Look what you done," the woman said. "Heathen."

The old man spit in the general direction of the flame.

"Pork," he said.

The corpse was gently oozing.

The woman blew her nose.

Rae put down the gun. "I believe we are next," she said.

The old man squinted at Rae. He wiped his needle with a triply phlegmy-looking rag.

Rae yanked a shirt, along with the body all but un-conscious inside it. "This here is Vern," she said.

"Hell," the old man said.

"It won't but a fever," Rae said.

"Won't do."

"Why not?"

"Can't be of service," the old man said.

"Why not, I said," Rae said.

"Basically," the old man said, "this fellow is human."

The woman had dropped to her fearsome knees. "Killer," she said.

"All the more reason," Rae said.

The line pitched forward with rancor.

"This fellow," the old man said to Rae, "is this some relation of yours?"

"Call him whatever you want," Rae said.

At some point, something ill-defined was passed from Rae's stained dress. Needless to dwell on what followed. Rae shut her eyes.

The old man slapped himself, said, "Good as new."

"Vern?" Rae said. "Vern? Do you know me?"

"Cured," the old man said.

The eye whites were stitched through with blood. "Where is my wallet at?" he, the newly woke, demanded of Rae.

A woman with a hen in a sack came forth.

"Never mind," the old man said. "Don't owe me so much as a stick."

"Let's go," Rae said.

"My cash," he said. "What is that thing? It looks to have died."

"Heathen," the kneeling woman said.

Gnats began to congregate.

"Come on," Rae said.

The old man said, "You're all shook up. Go get some shut-eye, you."

IN stations where the lighting was dusty and northern, falling through a high, stained glass—always a bench, an old stuck clock, walleyelike, always an indeterminate voice, remote, cracked: a.m., p.m., naming the cities that nobody went to; always a paper, local and disabused of news; stubs, ash, mites, a sprinkle of if-it-rains or if-it-sleets or if-it-snows or if-it-hails old salt, in churches, all denominations, better empty, dark loft, dark nave, in airless buses, qualmishly praying for a window, one clean sink, in castoff crates with room enough for outsize limbs, damp, always damp, even deep in the shadow of somebody's dwelling, overhung and luminous, this is where they lay themselves, he and she, to rest. "Sleep," he said. "Sleep easy." In fields, he watched the sky, shot through, he said, with stars or with the moon, and in the morning with the planets, or the near northern lights, or with the early-morning snow. Early as she stirred, he and she were gone.

They were given to things: eating whatever whenever

wherever. Of course they were. Who wouldn't be? Rae emptied her pockets. Bit chapped lips. Hers like his. She reassessed. Reflected in the blade of a knife. Gently, she emptied other pockets. Lifted her chin. She was given to lifting a dress, a hat, a lady's lamb's wool coat—"Nice," she said—some pigskin gloves, a man's nice leather jacket. "Vern?" she said. "Look."

He wore the jacket open.

The northern air was fierce.

A village was given to borderline criminal activity. Order in a river town was called into question. A man who was said to have called himself Phil committed a thoroughly lawless murder. Rae, over breakfast—juice, slaw, ribs—wiped her mouth, said, "Mercy." She held up a badly doctored map. "Does this seem familiar?" she said.

He chewed.

He chewed some more.

She swallowed.

"This house," she said, "where is it?"

"Trust me," he said.

She was forking up drippings.

"Like I trust myself," she said. She lifted the fork, high as his mouth, said, "Bite?"

NAILS were in evidence. So were shingles, drainpipes gagged with ice.

"Hit," he said.

"My hands," she said.

"Hard," he said. "Your what?" The wind was in the

trees, in the reddening gnarls of his ears. "Do you hear me?" he said.

"No," she said.

"What?" he said. "You're holding that hammer like a girl."

She tightened her grip. "Lockjaw is what," she said. "That's what." The nails of her fingers were gray. The ladder was feeble. The nail she was tapping was a virulent color. Between her teeth, a nasty point was stuck.

"Stop it," he said.

She spat it, girl-like. "Likely we'll break our necks," she said.

"Why don't you wear your gloves?" he said.

"No," she said. "They'll spoil."

He righted a shingle, grunted.

"Some deal," she said. "Some job you went and got us." She was not given to working in this dangerous manner with her hands. She was not keen, she said, of hired employment.

She predicted splinters, and mutinous behavior.

The ladder shuddered.

"Rae?" he said. "We won't die broke. Look in that window."

Daylight was slipping.

"Yes?" she said.

"No one can see us," he said.

"What is this color trim?" she said, regarding a grander residence some small ways north. "What do you call it?"

"Red?" he said. "Rust?" he said. "Ruby glow?"

"Too late," she said. She was swinging the hammer

with feminine abandon. Something squawked. She strangled it. She stuffed her coat, her dress, herself. "Pick out what you want," she said.

"What's this?" he said, in rosy, dying light.

"Glass," she said. "A window."

"Not now," he said. "Not anymore."

A woman screamed. Shards glittered like the wintry landscape. Down went the sun. To judge by the sound, the woman was probably heavily running. "Thief," she screamed.

"Vern," Rae said.

"Brick?" he said.

"Hurry up," Rae said. "I think that woman wants her nails back."

"Stop," the woman screamed.

"Tessie," a man yelled, "give us some peace."

The woman screamed, "Murder! Help," she included.

Lights snapped into life.

Rae dropped the hammer. Raced.

The voice of another woman rose: "Police!" she cried. "Police! Doctor! Officer!"

Someone cried, "Tessie! Bill! Lucette!"

There were men and there were women in the darkening road, and feathers and bed things, shards, shoes, gloves, rats, lint, tar, fleece, scraps, twigs, and indescribable splinters of trim.

"Rae?"

"What?"

"Run," he said.

"I am," she said.

A violent whistle.

Black. Cold black. Combustible black, ruinous foot-felt, lumpy black. Stars were in abundance. The screaming was fading. He and she were moving combustibly, blackly. "What am I touching?" she said.

"Guess," he said.

She screamed.

"I heard that," he said.

"Coal," he said. "Likely."

"I never liked a train," she said. "Did you?"

Nighttime pounded by. He seemed to try to stand. He slumped. Whatever was beneath them both was shifting. Surely, there were smells—the smell of a thing like coal, like grain, like carbon, the smell of a lake or body of water, out of view, unseeable, or something like the liquid night itself. Night birds were shrilling. Goatsuckers, she called them. Nightjars. Drops softly fell.

"Did I?" he said.

"Did you what?" she said.

"Like a train," he said.

She offered him something. "Eat," she said.

A warming filled his hand. He held it.

"Vern?" she said.

"What now?" he said.

"Do you think there's a heaven?"

Under his nose, he held it still.

"Ask me what I think," she said.

"Do you want to hear something true?" he said.

"Don't know," she said. "Depends." She crossed her arms. Her knees she brought up chestwise.

His jaw was slowly working. "I never liked to travel," he said.

"That so?"

"It is."

"Myself, I would say it depends," she said.

"Would you?"

"I would."

"What on?"

"How far," she said.

"To where?" he said.

She expelled her breath.

"Bad answer," he said.

"What am I eating?" he said.

"Something or other," she said.

"Which?" he said.

"I'm stiff as a board," she said. "I'm stiff as a clapboard house's boards."

"Sweet," he said. He wrapped her in his jacket despite she wore a coat. He whistled—a shallow, languid sound.

"Is it morning?" she said.

"No," he said.

"Now?" she said.

"Yes," he said.

"My gloves," she said, patting. "Look. Are you looking? I think I've gone and lost them."

He had finished eating.

"Don't sweat it," he said.

THE woman had a stove, stove-in, in the middle of the ramble of her yard. She had pumps for gas, for air, with icy nozzles stiffly hanged, drinks for sale so cold, the glass was crazed. She had tricky chairs, a pillow sprouting feathers. She had wrenches and marbles, selected appliances, haywire toasters, fryers furred with some contagion, claw-foot tubs, assorted seamy clothes. She had no arms. None at all. Rooted in her chin, she had what looked to be whiskers.

"Ma'am," he said, "good day."

"It is," the woman said.

"People call me Jordan," he said. "Call me Jordan."

"Do they?" she said.

"Like the river," he said.

"Rae," Rae said.

"Mrs. Hatch," the woman said. "Like Mrs. Hatch."

"Missus," Rae said. "Nice place."

"Onliest shopping around," Mrs. Hatch said.

"Onliest anything else," Rae said.

The land seemed placid, embalmed. Flat-out and trackless.

"Jordan," Rae said, "ask her."

"What day is it?" he said.

The eyes went dark.

"Missus?" he said.

"Jack," she said. "You think the world was made for you to come and rule it, don't you?"

"Sunday?" he said.

"Don't know as I know," she said. "Don't know as it rightly matters."

"Guess not," he said.

"Thursday or Tuesday or some such," she said.

"What about Wednesday?"

"Either, or," she said.

"What all is this?" Rae said.

"Not Sunday," Mrs. Hatch said. "I'm working up a powerful sweat."

There were barrels full of dresses—women's and children's, dolls', too. In one of the barrels, a small cat rolled. Cat-eyed. Lifeless. Stockings with tassles. A shoe.

"I might have been wanting gloves," Rae said.

"Where do you keep the cash?" he said.

"One at a time," said Mrs. Hatch. "Don't know as I carry gloves."

"So where is the till?" he said.

"Jack," she said.

"I told you once," he said. "Jordan. Like the river."

"Maybe a ribbon," she said to Rae. "Or maybe a frilly nightie?"

"Move," he said.

Her sleeves moved, drifty and weightless. The weather seemed entirely given to change.

"Who is he to you?" Mrs. Hatch asked.

"Just do what he says," Rae said. She was fingering man-size shirts. Dressylike. Over the pockets, names of men were roundly sewn, silky and cursive.

"Move," he said, louder.

Mrs. Hatch yawned. "Is this some kind of stickup?" she said.

"Yes, ma'am," he said.

"Well, where is your weapon at?" she said.

"Don't know as I need it," he said. "What's to stop us from robbing you blind?"

"Him," she said.

"Who?" he said.

"Our Lord," she said.

"Whose?" he said. "Jesus'?"

"I've got me a knife," Rae said.

"I warn you," Mrs. Hatch said. "I aim now to pray."

"How?" he said.

"Easy—for your soul," she said.

"How can you," he said, "without you have arms?"

"Vern," Rae said.

"Damn it, Rae," he said. "Don't let her know."

Wind whipped up. A dark cat snapped across the yard. Leaves blew sideways from nowhere, wrongly formed.

"Don't think I don't know," Mrs. Hatch said. "I know you. I knowed you the minute I first laid eyes."

Bibs lifted, defiled, into the air.

Rae covered her ears. "Mercy," she said. She was not making predictions, she said. "Jordan," she said, "Hey, River," she said, "come on."

He was spilling over barrels, a gas pump, toasters, frisking Mrs. Hatch.

"Heavenly Father," she said as wet wind roared.

"Save it," he said. "Nothing," he said. "Rae," he said. "She don't got so much as a dime."

Rae sat herself down on the riotous earth. There was something she was holding by the tail. "Missus," she said. "Please," she said, "do you think you could give us directions?"

THE valley loomed stark and gloomy, dwellingless. A dented-in basin. A miserable trough. For days, they'd eaten ice. Nights, they'd eaten ice. Her hair was iced with ice. He had, as you would surely imagine, an unshaved chin, which was not without ice.

It chafed her, she said.

Birds were lying stiff-winged and bent-necked.

"Don't eat them," he said.

"Why north?" she said.

"What?" he said.

"Why not south?" she said.

His breathing was audible.

"Don't you rightly wonder?"

"No."

"Why not?"

"Fact," he said.

"What fact?" she said.

"Fact is," he said, "this is the way we been heading. Women," he said.

"There's no one here," she said. "Not one lone soul."

"Us," he said. "We are."

She lifted her hair. "I ache," she said. "Go carry these yourself." She was pulling out shirts from out of her person, stitched: Daryl, Red, Jack.

"What are those?" he said.

"What do you think they are?" she said. "Yours."

"Mine?" he said.

"Who else?" she said.

"Stole?" he said.

"You know I don't like that word," she said. "She didn't so much as look."

"I see," he said. "So where will I wear them?"

An owl lay busted. Trees began to screech, tormented by the elements.

"I don't expect I know," she said.

A hawk stretched boldly, deadly on the earth.

"Night bird," she said.

"Vulture," he said.

"I never killed a thing," she said.

"Lucky you," he said.

"I didn't," she said.

He smothered a yawn.

"Oh, that," she said.

They stood there, stunned with ice.

"Where all do we sleep?" she said.

"You'll sleep," he said.

"Where?" she said.

"Hereabouts."

"Don't step on that," she said. "We'll need to set a fire."

A bullet lit on by.

"Rae?" he said.

"Don't call me that."

"Why?" he said. "Do you happen to have any coal on yourself?"

"Why would I?" she said. "I'm surprised you even asked." She was toeing the hawk. "Will it burn?" she said.

"Straight up," he said.

She sat. And sat and sat, devoured in shadow. "Got us as much as a match?" she said. "A piece of sorry flint?"

THE house was all in light. Expansive, pillared. Solid, and seemingly impenetrably windowed. Deliriously trimmed. It seemed to be growing.

Her fingers were fat, red, raw. Her knuckles bled from knocking.

A crack.

A glint.

A woman. A feathery rug. The woman wore a night-dress, nightcap, gloves. She was holding a candle. Lit. White. Her hair was white. Her face was lit and in some brutal way, Vern's.

"Mother?" Rae said.

A sound like air, a hiss.

The woman shrank. The candle dropped. Gloves were at her eyes—Rae's eyes. "Do I know you?" she said.

"It's me," Rae said.

The rug began to spit. Night things were searing. Dress, cap, bone. "Murder," she whispered.

"Doll," he said. His chin was at her ribs, at her mouth. A heat was at her throat. "Where are you?" he said.

"Do I know you?" she said.

"HOW do I know what you know?" he said.

She was stealing from a pitiful tree. "You don't," she said. She bit.

Over the mountains and into the caverns, out of the earth vents, steaming, cold, around invented cityscapes, ghostly in their industry, a steam stack, a house drenched brightly in flame, past nestings of darkness, red-eyed and hungry, a graveyard where someone had lifted the wings, had tampered with the earth, had beaten with the body, on ragged tongues of shoreline, clacking into rivers, streaming, clogged, with carcasses bobbing and sinking and bobbing, pockets full of sweat, tears, clenchy little fingers, smoothing, crying, stealing into merciless, lucid afternoons, simply, the two of them went.

And went. And went some more.

Starved, scared, frozen up and boiled down, pocked, knifed, cursed, drowned, scratched out and bulleted are ways they could have died.

They did not die.

They limped. His stride grew noticeably shorter. Their shoes were only holes. "Our feet seem to carry us nowhere," she said.

A small wind carried the smell of a season.

"Does this seem familiar?" she said.

"Let me think," he said.

He squatted.

She squatted. Brittle.

Tall trees arched across the road, intertwining in a ceiling overhead.

"This house," she said. She wiped her mouth.

Blood was on his lip.

"What of it?" he said.

"Do you think we maybe missed it?"

"Could," he said.

"When?" she said.

Sunlight was streaking through the branches. Something was flitting.

"Don't suppose I know," he said. He buttoned the thin-skinned shreds of his jacket. Crossed tight his arms.

"You think we were ever inside?" she said. "Vern," she said. "Whoever you are. Could a person be there and not know?"

"Here is what I think," he said. He stood again. "There must be someplace else."

No one would stop them. This he predicted. No one was going to give them away. "North will turn to south," he said.

"It will?" she said.

"It will," he said.

Old now, expectant, they went on bloody claws of feet—step, step, step, step—a hard, abiding prayer on the surface of the earth.

SECRETS

OF

BREEDING

"THIS house in August sweats," the man says.

"Crawls," the woman says.

"Oh, flies," the man says, "flies," and he is moving his hand in the direction of the woman or of something that the woman can not see. "I can live with the flies," he says.

"Something's living in the wood," the woman says. "Infested," she says. "And it is nothing sweating."

"Drip," the woman's daughter says, but softly from the kitchen. She is feeding the plants, which she does in this house, and they are droopy in the heat.

Little pitchers is a saying of the woman's.

It is true, this much: The man and the woman and the woman's daughter have been all summer catching and swatting with various swatters, slapping at the walls, the slitty louvered doors, skin. Nights, they roll the news. In the mornings, there are markings on the moldings, wingy and smeared, something drying on the valance eyelet. There's a pucker in a cornice. Things have been known to disappear, too. Thin flickings can be heard against the fans' slick blades, a hiss and sizzle from the porch, where a bare bulb is burning. Clues, hints is what the daughter of the house has said—"There's a hole in my sock and in the dark, who knows?"

"Bees," the woman says to the man. "Even bees. And what can you expect?" the woman says. "She is always overeager with a window, slamming and banging, and the screens in disrepair. And you," the woman says to the man. "You, too."

"But this pilling and fungus," the man says. "Look."

It is true, in a manner of fact, this: There's a tic in the pipes, a spastic lapse, and the clock, which is made to run on last year's yams—a hobby of a certain party in this house—is sluggish, losing seconds on the hour, in the sweep of an inch.

A bird in the bush is a saying of the man's.

"Please," the daughter of the pastime says. She is in from the kitchen with a flash of flashy leaves in a pot. She says, "The coleus is fragile, molting. Mom," she says.

"There is nothing for dinner," the woman says. "The skin of a potato, soup to peas, there is nothing I would care to cook in this house anymore," the woman says. "And do you know why?" the woman says. "Guess."

"Greens don't molt," the man says. "Hair."

"Bristles," the woman says. "You—you have dirt beneath your fingernails," the woman tells the daughter. "Everything is nibbled or wilted, spoiled."

"Something cold. A carrot," the man says. "Mushrooms. How about a salad?"

"Scales?" the woman's daughter says.

"Yes," the woman says. "There's a buzz. You would have to be deaf."

"What else?" the daughter says. "What molts?"

"Fur," the man says.

"Horns," the woman says.

Don't toot your horn is a saying, too, but the walls in this house cannot talk, of course.

The daughter has ears in her head. She says, "A feather?"

"What kind?" the man says.

"Down," the woman says. "Because it breathes."

DISTURBANCES

IN

THE

NIGHT

IT began with a sneeze. Whose? His? Hers? Theirs? The room in which the babies slept was lit, but only lowly, from a socket. There were cockleshells and ruffles. Nothing telling. Soft. The dog was snoring audibly. Linoleum was curling in the kitchen. Was there something coolly humming? Something dripped. Blew. Yes?

Ah, house!

God's blessings were cribbed, exchanged.

A light was switched.

Then came sounds of running water, paws, a thump.

"Is that you?"

"Who else?"

There were flounces, edges, cues a spouse discerns. Which?

"Sssshhh," said she, wife.

He coughed.

Trees, iced, clinked the bubbled glass. Wind whined. A cup was filled.

Over. Again.

Repeat. Repeat. Repeat.

Splash. Lo!

Now let there be towels. Let there be cloths for ablution, for sopping the excess—his, hers—piled and plush, initialed. Done. Money newly minted. Done. A flourishing of service at a snap—the bridal gravy boat, the creamer at your elbow; let us spare no expense on flowing lace. Oh, let fluted crystal ring! Done. Done. Whites talced, a hem, something swishy and medicinal.

"Cold," said she of hers, "so," and sipped.

"Too," said he, and he, house's mister, gargled, spat.

Did something rattle in a chest?

Hope lodged.

A dental utterance was deemed stuck.

"Do? Till?"

"Till?"

When?

And did said chest presume to be whose?

This is too much to ask.

He—cleared—dispensed, unplugged, harrumphed.

"Please," said she, parental. There were wee little ears and after all, the time: dead of night, said she; the early morning, he—both at once, for once.

Next, taps, scuffs.

She, waxing prudent, noted chill to factor in, responsibilities, credentials.

He was fully vested. Why? Oh, his aching brain! There were theories and offspring, vectors to vex, the voweled bundles versus bills, said he, diapers, drool, the urgent issues of the day to be examined and discussed.

A nose was nosing rudely.

There were standards, contexts, the slow, wound roads to parenthetical concerns. (Whose? Yours?) And let us have ellipses. . . . There was mercury to shake down and tongue. Ah . . . ah . . .

"Depress."

Teeth.

A haunch.

A touch.

"Feel this forehead"—he.

"Patience"—she.

"Don't scratch"—addressed to whose best friend? A thrushy coating on the mouth's sore roof, remaindered phrases, a slight taste of sand (a foretaste, too, of something to infinitively swallow, slather).

He: Is this normal?

She (wife-ish, squinting): Blankety blank point blank. This suspicion carried over under quilts; hasty paddings, back, forth, a ruffle fluffed, a suckled toast—gesundheit!—the pillows cased and found to be infected.

Heads. Tails.

Unrest, unrest, unrest.

The seconds seemed to toss, the walls to flex.

Something skittered: in the attic, said she; in the crawl space, he, to be exact, or quite likely in the plumbing or circuits, or something in ferment, or the dog, dreaming doggedly, fervently, in slavish devotion to who knew what?

Cries. A howl. A wail.

The sound of keening.
Oh, could there be no containing this house?

GOD spare us this house!

AND let us leave a mark above the door to save our place.

LET us wander on the slow roads away. Let us travel brittle fields. Let us harvest the fallow, huddle, tarry, suck our blackened roots. Let us forage in the orchards, tap the family trees. Let us milk our bright machines and find them gleaming, spent. Let us shiver in the forest. Let us march across the creeks, groaning with the effort, the rigid beds of oceans, cracking polar caps.

For this chill becomes climactic, systemic.

Logic snaps. Projection renders only goosey flesh, extrapolation the same, the same.

Steps lock.

Glass breaks.

The gelid borders shut.

An ill-considered touch can cost a finger, a tongue; a bit of metal, a life.

It is too cold for charms.

A child has died wanting in, knocking wood. . . .

"LET'S look," said she.

"Let's sleep," said he.

"You look," said she.

"Why me?" said he.

"In the morning; it is nothing, the dog," said he.

"The babies?"—she.

"What babies?"—he.

"Stop whining"—he.

"Is that you?"—she.

"IS that you?". . .

THE dog has left a stain.

A drainpipe is dripping.

Must we help ourselves? Listen, the babies will not be of service. Let us assume: The babies must still be the babies, or else other babies—hungry, wet, diseased.

The pillows must be plumped. The furnace must be stoked. The mister and the missus must not have gotten better. Let us think of them as worse. Why not? It is a matter of time, in any event. Will they claim not to know us? Do you blame them? Think. They are wheezing in bed. They are chattering, doubting. No? Yes. They will never agree.

We have nowhere to sit.

Something has contracted in the throat.

The sheets must be warm. The lips must be split. The knees must be broken.

They will not reveal their names.

Who will see us? Know us? Who will sniff us out? We are not accounted for.

The first blood is ours.

UP

THE

OLD

GOAT

ROAD

WE are here on the peninsula, where pie is made from scratch and the goats are getting fatter on a nearby roof. It is an upwind roof. This is industry, my father says. Company, my sister says. This is not the dells. All the supper clubs are shut or tight. The falls are somewhere else we have not been. Overhead is where it's lusher, fresh—green above this hard-luck thumb. But the goats, my sister says, look overwarm. The water is our neighbor, and what washes up is sorry or worse.

There is the smell of the quick.

My mother is cooking in the kitchen again, and I do not know what. Something is chopping. Something is chirping. Something is black in a tree, and blue. A piano must be playing at a distance, someone four and twenty singing, someone whistling for dinner, someone cutting a rug, someone sweeping, and rinsing every dish in the sink. The kettle is on. The timer is off. Efficiency, my mother says, is why she keeps the pans, the pots, the spatulas and spoons, the metal platter for the fish, the cream clotting in the bottle, the needlepoint sampler, tongs, tins, mitts, and all the spices of our life on a hook.

We children are not children. We are sister and sister, face front and center, buttoned mother-of-pearl. Mother's oven is Dutch. The rattle of the boil is a sound we sisters prefer to ignore. We are waiting on the weather, my sister says. We are waiting for a fit like a fine kid glove. We are waiting for a higher tide to roll in.

It is a hook my mother says she nailed herself.

An unrelated rumor has been hanging in the air.

My mother keeps a basket by the door with nothing in it. It is there for the season, my mother says. She says, Go and fetch your father. He is salting the beach.

A job is a job. This could not be simpler.

But my sister and I are slow and slowest. We are in the wrong year. Our father is never in the place we expect. Father sickness-and-health, he is chewing the breeze. He is checking what is greener on the other side. He is butter through our fingers. Gone.

The rumor is bearing on the burial mounds. It is the clatter of change. There is talk of heads of arrows switching hands up the Old Goat Road. Somebody is selling precious pennies, it is said, and crooked corn. Somebody is selling beads of sweat, a little Pepsi in a cup. Somebody is marking down the souvenir bones of Paul Bunyan and his blue ox, Babe.

We do not investigate ourselves.

The stitching in the kitchen says nothing, is only p's and q's, is out-of-date.

It is winter already and the ice is full of fish, my mother says. We have the recipes engraved on a laminated log. We have lanyards and all-purpose holiday plums. We have edible leaves. We have drawstring hoods. This is smart, my mother says. But we are winded and it smells like snow.

All the stiffs are frozen stiff, my sister says. She is waiting on tables that are empty. She is waiting on a headdress, a puff-puff, a tepee for two. My mother's hair has turned to silver and we are scraping by.

I am making a crust. I am fluting the edge.

My father is sighted up the hill and in the road and on the lake. But it is never him. The party line is busy. There's a message in a bottle. A ship is on a shore.

My sister has begun to misremember. In the interest of time, my sister says, she has started seeing double. She is slugging the port. She is carrying a tune south across the border.

My mother has a suitor with a range.

There is a legend on the map.

There is something boiling over.

There has been a drowning.

We have prints. We have a photo of the Mona Lisa on a ring for keys. This is not Chicago. We have cherries by the peck.

There are stars for lying under.

There are stones.

My sister is impossible to call. We have gone too

far. We are no longer listed. They have changed the ex-
change. The poor old goat, my mother says, is gouty and
spent.

But we are somewhere else. We are always somewhere
else. We are in this plangent earth. We are going up the
road. We are standing on the roof of the world, facing off.

MIGRATION

GEESE came. Dark as the loam of fertile lands, they came, the sky incessant. In the hard fields bladed brown, no further crop would fill the woven horns of fall. The trees were plainly picked. The ridges of the soil held the feathers of the frost. Thick past marsh, low above farmland, the flat-lying places of rattly dwellings, clapboard dwellings, all dark clouds were geese. There were no formations.

"Hush," a woman said.

"Patience," a woman said.

A woman said, "Hope, look up."

This was in the time of the Indian corn tied tight to doors with dry stalks. The doors had mats of husk. Dark jars filled the cellars. A pressure could be felt at the temples of the women. Beds were lumpy. Rooms were cold, the floors fast-whisked.

Men were in pursuit. The men had boots and firstborn sons. The sons had dogs to point. Meat was scarce. Skins cracked. Every kettle sang.

In the butter-lit kitchens, the women stood to do with hand and knife the things that women stood to do. The wind was in the curtains, sinkside. There were daughters in the leaves.

This is what the youngest child knew: The geese stirred talk. The hands of women floated. A mother was a woman whose rings caught a curious light.

Loose at a threshold, the child was a flicker—back of an ankle, under a step, awry, soft cheek to slat. She was damply jumpered. Her hair fell to curls of the shade of the ground, of wood, of the hair of her father's chest. He had loaded his shotgun. The child quickened to muted noises, pulses in the walls.

A syllable could echo.

The father might have whispered.

The names of the child were the names of the dead. Out of the ether, into the night, the mother's broken cries had flown.

"Junior," a woman said.

"No," the mother said. "Hope Hope."

The windows were jimmied. The sheets were twice-boiled. A woman said, "Prudence." The knees of a woman were reddened and scarred. There were moons in the floors. The rugs were rag, beaten. The violence of touch was at a hem, most stubbornly waddled to get to.

This was an issue of friction.

The child paid no mind; the women said Little Miss.

There were designated corners for speaking in tones.

Weaned she was, the women said. She was no rashy drooler, Miss Hope Hope. No gobby bib and teat. She was unrestful. Eyes to where she mightn't ought to be, the women said. What a body would think!

There were speckles in the air.

The father of the child had licked a sturdy finger, raised it, tested for conditions. His was the smell of straps and hoods, of flannel—his, his skin. He had been brooding. His smells were in the quilts.

Fat pads were in nooks and in shadowy alcoves in all the abodes.

The daughters knelt to wax. They were tricky and preening. Nights, the daughters pursed their lips and stole. The dark was a gradation. Their frenzy was invisible. An index finger to a daughter smelt of brine. Their smocks smelt of earth. Under the nails of the daughters were splinters and crescents of blood.

The leanings of men, the women said, left stains. The ordering of sons was not reliable. Chairs rocked back dug ruts, the women said.

"Patience," a man said.

Everybody waited on the sky's murky bounty.

HUSK, sheaf, reed, twig, thread—the women wove. They hummed. Blood was their relation. Callused and tender, thickened to a split, the hands would not relent.

Picture the gravy, the women said, the wine, the wings. Think of the abundance to preserve. Think of the steam! How the marrow would glisten!

The daughters scavenged crusts.

The women laid cloth. Horn and grace, basket and music, russet and candle; palm, palm, hymn—the service would shine, the women said. Under the tables, nestling paws-to-toes, loyal, the dogs would have plenty.

"Faith, yes, do you hear?" a woman said.

The women were named for the things not seen.

Drawing with the shadows was the province of the

child. Fingers were her implement, laced, her thumbs, all of the whole of herself. She was as tall as the knobs. Adorable texture was what she was—the nub of a mother's chenille, the warp, the glowy, got-to shock. She was a wick. She was soft as paraffin sealing over jars. Hers was the searing incision. She was a beam, a funnel for the light. She was thrashing and thrashing on the rafters. She was enormous.

"Mama?" she said.

A woman said, "Hope?"

The names of the daughters were doubled.

A handle was braided.

"Hope?" a woman said. "Hope Hope?"

Report was expected.

The daughters were somewhere, a rustle and trill.

Patience was called for.

"Mama," the child said. "Look."

"Herself is in the door," a woman said.

The youngest child's mother sucked the color from a long, wet cut.

DOGS sniff.

A father shows a son how to see in the blind, in dusk. He teaches a son to shoot, to track, to memorize positions of the planets. "Look up," a father says. A father says, "Junior."

Junior says, "Boy."

A chill seeps in through mitten and flannel, fur, through sacks for the storing of game, through matted, ruined down.

Nose to the quilts, the last-born trembles, snuffles, learning through the skin and from the air. She will master consonants, the hard hearts of words. Her curls will be shorn. "Papa?" she will say. Yearning is inbred. Longing for the missing will be mercilessly easy.

Patience is the mother. The name is assumed. Patience will clench the etched face of a stone, tread stately on the braids of fraying rugs. She will make the most of a morsel.

There will be salves and rags in the pocket of Patience's apron, an anxious pleat.

There will be a bullet.

BONE, joint, tissue, flounce, dwindling larder—the kitchens throbbed.

"The walls have ears," a woman said.

The days were clingy. Aprons hung. The windows were strange.

"Mind you," a woman said.

"I am deep-down to the wrist," a woman said.

In song and in fever, the women's voices rose. They were not distinguished. The names were immaterial.

A gobbet on the counter was a live thing.

"Salt it down," a woman said.

"Scratch a day off," a woman said.

Ribs could be numbered.

The dogs were retrievers. Fluid stopped a bullet. A woman called for Prudence. No silky, glossy nap, the women said—surely the sons would have grown. "Fetch" was an order. A dog could suck a yolk. Junior was a son. The Third was a son.

The dogs were golden. The weather was something. The men were presumed to be expert in direction.

"Where are they now?" a woman said.

HOPE Hope loomed. Her fingers were cocked. Her nails would scratch. She was not so young, the women said. Was she not theirs, by blood and cycle, sex and will? Her names were carved, inscribed in dust. A rub of an eye, she was, the women said. She snooped. Miss Miss Hope Hope— ingenuous Patience's—trespassed under the beds.

"Simple," a woman said.

"Strip off the ears," a woman said.

Copper was scoured. The Indian kernels were mightily cooked.

The moon was full.

The daughters smelt of tallow and of pointed disobedience. They had broken jars.

The men would have their version.

The power of report might burn in the eyes, the arms might grow past cuffs, the cold raise bumps, and might could the straps might bite, a woman said.

The cider was hazed.

Teeth marked a bullet.

Reunion was long past due.

"HUSH."

The women bathed a forehead. They swabbed the dull lids of eyes, lips, the sexless neck, the hollow and the rattle of the throat.

Psalms were offered.

The women told stories, beginning with "Once," beginning with rain, beginning with "In the beginning."

They slipped off their rings and they stacked them on spikes, the women did. Clocks were set back, according to ordinance. Tapers could burn and burn by a bed.

The light was charged.

A story went about in which a roof had been lifted. "A roof could be lifted," a woman said.

"Might could," a woman said.

The walls were weak. The tables were preserved in perpetual chill. The shape of another could have settled in the ticking.

The daughters were swollen.

"Think of the steam," a woman said.

Coins were warmed in palms for eyes, for the moment when the fluttering ceased.

Row, tier, palm, branches of the tree of the begotten, rock-walled cities of the named and the dead—boundaries yield.

Mother and Father, the violence of Hope Hope Hope—always they are beckoning.

Always we are yearning to be borne.

TWO

IF

BY

SEA

WHAT the girl could see that morning were the shining northern lights. She could see her breath, drifting, and the moon, milky. The girl made a bowl with both hands for blowing into. She looked for Venus. Found it. She did not know the time.

The ground beneath her shoe boots had been hard, with hard snow. The girl's steps were cautious. She was testing, toeing, slipping in inches from land. The river ice was thin and growing thinner. Just before the girl went under, she could hear it crack.

SHE would recall, the girl thought, that the place had had an echo. Tile. People. Someone brushing her hair, damp, back from her face, someone telling her she must take the liquid, which was warm in the glass, and thick. She would remember, too, the taste of something undissolved, and swallowing.

THERE was heat coming up from beneath the dash and the mother's voice, raised, questioning the girl, the mother asking the girl why she had done such a thing as she had done, the mother driving with the girl past other people's houses, nothing on the porches, wreaths on the doors, past fencing falling half down from too much weather, silos, nothing, cords of wood, the mother asking the girl, who was nosebleeding into a kerchief, why—yes, why—past beat-up metal boxes for the mail, flagged, rusted shut, or opened, dark inside; split trees, a squirrel in the road, the road, and the girl with her one hand free, drawing and drawing on the last wet left on the window: wavy shapeless shapes.

Then the mother was telling the girl some something, some story taking place when the mother was the age the girl was now, or close, and the girl just closed her eyes and made a sound, and the mother said, "Look," said, "maybe we had better off go somewhere."

"Like where?" the girl said.

"For the day," the mother said.

And the girl said, "Right, what else?" She said, "I need another rag here."

"Pinch," the mother said.

"I can't," the girl said.

"Try again," the mother said. "Keep an eye out for a station."

"I'm thirsty," the girl said.

"Don't push your luck," the mother said.

"Let me tell you a story," the mother said.

The girl smeared the window with a sleeve, took a look out the sideview mirror. She tried to see through dried-on salt. "Back there," the girl said.

"It was a hole," the mother said. "In the earth. I was raised in this place."

"You missed it," the girl said.

"Didn't you know? She was buried in the earth alive," the mother said.

"Who was?" the girl said.

The mother said, "Eggs."

THE booth was missing stuffing. There were chips in the dishes. The smell the girl smelled was of coffee and frying.

The girl had asked a question.

"Knock on wood," the mother said. "How's your nose?"

"In one piece," the girl said.

"Eat your toast, then," the mother said.

The girl said to tell her was it blood or by marriage. She watched the mother eat.

"I don't like this," the girl said.

The mother said, "Then leave it on your plate."

SHE would recall, the girl thought, at the bottom of the drink, thinking that the light had played a trick.

"BUT it was only shoulder-high," the girl was saying. She was standing in the doorway doing buttons.

"Not so," the mother said. "And it was hollow—that was the trouble."

"Push," the girl said.

"I thought you had a hat," the mother said. "Coming in. I could have sworn it."

THE preserve where the mother and the girl were walking was dense with trees.

Breathing hurt.

There was underfoot crunching the girl could hear, and the small sounds of forage.

There was this for miles.

"She burned her flesh," the mother said. "On the rope, which was frayed."

"What flesh?" the girl said.

The mother said, "Pulling."

"She got out?" the girl said.

"But you said," the girl said.

"This is where she is," the mother said. "Right here in this brush."

THE mother and the girl were some distance from the house by the river where they lived. There were jingles on the radio. The sun was sinking. The girl kept turning the dial. Got more of the same, the same, static. "There's nothing on," the girl said.

"It's early still," the mother said. And then the mother told the girl how, at night, on clear nights, a person might catch any far-off thing, from who knew where.

About the Author

*Dawn Raffel is a native of Wisconsin and was
graduated from Brown University. She is married,
is the mother of Brendan, and is fiction editor
at* Redbook.

A Note on the Type

*The text of this book is set in Garamond No. 3. It is
not a true copy of any of the designs of Claude
Garamond (1480–1561), but an adaptation of
his types, which set the European standard for two
centuries. It probably owes as much to the designs of
Jean Jannon, a Protestant printer working in Sedan
in the early seventeenth century, who had worked with
Garamond's romans earlier, in Paris, and who was
denied their use because of the Catholic censorship.
Jannon's matrices came into the possession of the
Imprimerie Nationale, where they were thought to
be by Garamond himself, and so described when the
Imprimerie revived the type in 1900. This particular
version is based on an adaptation by Morris
Fuller Benton.*

*Composed by Dix, Syracuse, New York
Printed and bound by Quebecor Printing,
Fairfield, Pennsylvania
Designed by Iris Weinstein*